APOSTASY RISING

END TIMES CHRONICLES SEASON 1
EPISODE 2

J. A. BOUMA

EmmausWay
PRESS

CHAPTER 1
TRIPOLITANIA. AD 2123.

"The Lord Jesus, on the night he was betrayed, took a loaf of bread," Deacon Zakaria Mwanyanyi said with a nervous tremor, both hands grasping the precious, sacred loaf of Christ's body in front of him with reverent care and trying his best not to drop it.

Burnt orange light from the evening sun reflecting off from the Mediterranean Sea just outside the ancient walls of the Tripolitanian church streamed through the windows lining the nave in thick ribbons, catching the incense still hanging heavy in the great hall of stone and steel that had served thousands of believers since the dawn of the early Church. He took in a deep breath, the spicy scent of the burnt frankincense steadying his nerves for the sacred ritual. The resin obtained from balsam trees for over two millennia also reminded the young minister of the deeply held traditions that still guided Ichthus despite the seismic changes that had hammered and honed the world outside those walls over the centuries. The ones born through the ravages of nuclear war and biological contagions; and through the Earth's groanings under the climatic shifts dubbed Armageddon; and through technological progress into space and political changes wrought through the Great Reckoning.

Through it all, the historic traditions and beliefs of Ichthus held the Church steady. And it was these traditions which Zakaria was a caretaker after taking his place a year ago alongside Father Alexander Zarruq in a long line of under-shepherds of the Great Shepherd succeeding Saint Peter as Christ's vicars on Earth.

Thank you, Lord Christ, for the privilege of stewarding your broken body and shed blood, he prayed silently. *And for the privilege of shepherding your flock that is about to consume these memory-markers. May you steady my spirit and guide my hands...*

Zakaria had hoped Father Zarruq would have returned by now to relieve him of the responsibility to carry on the sacred ritual. He had abandoned him several days ago after receiving a message from the Ministerium taking him away on urgent business, leaving him to serve in his stead—which included taking on the very public responsibility of leading Mass. But he was no Father Zarruq. He was always a nervous wreck in front of people, much more preferring behind-the-scenes pastoral care to the on-the-stage kind he was forced into assuming at the priest's delay.

But he allowed himself a small dose of pleasure serving the children of Christ in this manner, feeling privileged to be able to offer the memory-markers of Christ's payment for their sins and offer of eternal life through his sacrifice on the cross. The Lord Jesus sure knew they needed them, given the trials and tribulations that life had thrown their way in recent months.

And it was Zakaria who came bearing the sustenance of the Bread of Life for the precious saints arrayed before him.

A smile curled upward as his eyes began to wander across the nave, his hands still holding the loaf of Christ before him as his mind became lost in the sacred gravity of the moment.

They first locked onto Phoebe, who was seated in the front.

Named after the first-century deacon who bore the letter to Christians living in Rome written by Saint Paul, having read it to them and then explained its theological meaning, she certainly lived up to her namesake as a sturdy, steadying theological voice in the church—the matron of the parish if there ever was one. He knew how much the ancient ritual meant to her as someone who had darkened Death's threshold more than twice that year alone. The memory-markers of her faith fed her, nourished her, sustained her through the trials of this life.

She nodded and smiled at Zakaria. He nodded back and then continued making his way around the nave, landing on two parents and their son.

Miriam and Hosea were good and godly parents who had faithfully brought their son Isaiah up in the Church, seeing to his proper catechizing and baptism and guarding his faith as if it were their own. For most of the boy's years, he was sold out to Ichthus and on fire for Jesus. But Zakaria knew through Isaiah's confessions of late that the boy had been harboring great doubts and began to give himself over to sins he had once held at bay through the power of his faith. He wondered how much longer the boy who was almost a man might remain in that family pew near the back.

His face fell at the thought. He furrowed his brow slightly before brightening again and continuing on through the sacred space, names and faces and stories fueling his pastoral heart with love and admiration for the precious souls Christ had entrusted to his care—as dark and difficult as it had become for Ichthus since the Reckoning under the increasing pressures of Solterra and everyday citizens of the Republic.

Harmony above distinction...For Humanity! bleated the potentate Lucius Severus, a dog whistle for the masses to abandon the belief in the kind of singular faith and God in favor of a totalizing toleration of anything-goes beliefs and practices within the world community. Which the distinctiveness of Ichthus pushed back against with countercultural resistance.

Someone coughed, its echo snapping Zakaria back to the moment celebrating the holy Eucharist.

The warmth of embarrassment crept up his neck and flushed his cheeks. He smiled and bowed his head before raising it high and continuing the ritual that was meant to feed, nourish, sustain—even provoke—his people's faith.

He took a breath, then proclaimed, "And when he had given thanks, he broke the bread and said, *'This is my body that is for you. Do this in remembrance of me.'*"

He broke the unleavened bread in two and set the pieces down upon a gleaming silver platter resting on white linen lace that ran the length of the altar fashioned from sacred acacia wood, etched with gilt into leafy whorl patterns. Then he carefully clutched the heavy chalice weighed down by gold and the sacred wine it held, the memory-marker of Jesus Christ's shed blood for the forgiveness of sins.

Zakaria held forth the golden chalice before the gathered, faithful people of Christ, inviting them to taste and see the Lord's goodness found in the font that flowed freely from his hands and feet and side for their salvation from shame and guilt, for their rescue from sin and death. He paused, quietly thanking the Lord for the opportunity to lead the holy sacrament of communion in Father Zarruq's absence, as late arriving as he was.

He smiled widely and proclaimed, "In the same way, after supper he took the cup, saying, *'This cup is the new covenant in my blood; do this, whenever you drink it, in remembrance of me.'*"

Before setting the cup down upon the Eucharistic table to join the broken Body of his Lord, he continued with Paul's words from his first letter to the Church of Corinth, chapter eleven, raising the chalice above his head: *"For whenever you eat this bread and drink this cup, you proclaim the Lord's death until he comes."*

Amen, the crowd of Ichthus's faithful said in agreement.

"Amen," Zakaria said, setting the holy cup back on the altar. He went to offer the Eucharistic Prayer when an unholy roar at the back of the nave intercepted him.

A series of thunderous explosions ricocheted from the narthex along the ancient walls that bore the memory of Christ's Church stretching back to its existence. A choreography of stone chunks and pluming smoke exploded inside the sacred space at angry angles, sending a crescendoing wave of evil biting hard toward the high altar.

For Christ's under-shepherd, it all happened in slow-motion wickedness. From the stained glass Zakaria had helped clean each week blowing out in confetti-like shards to the black-and-red fireballs rolling over Miriam and Hosea and Isaiah on toward Phoebe. From the agonizing screams of confusion and pain to Christ's Body and Blood being overtaken by a menacing maw spawned from the loins of Satan himself—sending the priest flying high in a heaping pile of rubble and mangled limbs.

While Father Alexander Zarruq was returning home, nearing his precious parish down a path just outside, his precious parishioners—mothers and fathers, sons and daughters, believers and doubters, men and women—were consumed in a phantasmic show of fire and fury. A promised evil that had been hinted at for weeks was finally unleashed.

Terrorists had struck the Church of Tripolitania.

The fight for the faith of Ichthus had come home.

CHAPTER 2

THE FURIOUS EXPLOSION threw Father Alexander Zarruq to the ground hard on his back with wicked indifference. He was already disoriented from the tumble running into the figure darting down the path from his parish, his head throbbing from the exchange. Now his body ached that much worse.

And his brain froze with the realization that the series of cascading fireballs and billowing black smoke vandalizing the clear evening sky was the byproduct of a menacing evil overtaking his blessed church.

"*Noooo!*" Alexander screamed as he picked himself up off the ground and scrambled forward. A foot slipped on loose gravel, sending him back to the ground.

He cursed and pushed himself back off the ground, stealing a glance back to chance spotting the mysterious intruder he had collided with.

No one, nowhere.

He cursed again and ran toward his parish, a lancing pain in his right knee slowing him and forcing him to hobble along as fallen debris and a wicked smoke bloomed across his path. When he reached the top of the hill, the sight sucked the breath out of his lungs.

The small chapel where he had held daily prayers over the years was ripped from the side of the church, like a chunk of bread torn off the loaf for daily Mass. A maw of blackness with red and orange flaming fingers grasping up the side of one still-standing wall stood in its place, a window into the furnace raging inside. The roof at one end had collapsed, along with a portion of the wall on the west side of the cathedral. More flames were consuming what was left and belching black smoke obscured Alexander's view of the rest of the sacred structure. On the southern front, the two towers still stood with holy defiance, as they had through nearly two millennia. However, hungry flames already blackening the beige pockmarked stone threatened to bring them to their knees.

Sirens screamed in the distance from both land and air vehicles making their way to squash the fire before it overtook the neighborhood. Another concussive explosion deep in the belly of the demon-possessed church sent Alexander skidding to the ground. But he recovered and scrambled back toward the church in search of survivors. The one saving grace was his parsonage was yet untouched, though he cursed himself for being happy his house was safe while God's was being overrun by the powers of hell itself.

By the time he reached his church, a handful of parishioners had managed to flee the furnace. Others were dragging or carrying people with them as the structure burned and continued crumbling inside. Clearly the rumors that had been circulating the past week had just proven themselves true. And the terrorists had struck at the height of the evening Mass, ensuring maximum carnage and damage to Ichthus as it gathered for worship.

Alexander's head swam with anxiety and fear, but it had no time to gain purchase. He had to act. And fast.

He covered his nose and mouth with his sleeve and climbed

onto a heap of rubble that had been the southern wall of the small chapel just moments ago, making his way inside to search for survivors.

The ungodly sound of flapping flames and agonizing screams pressed in against his consciousness as he waded through the ruins. His foot caught on something. It slipped out from under him, sending him tumbling hard to the ground. He bashed his right shin on a large chunk of ancient brick and mortar, sending searing pain up his leg that combined with the fall he had taken earlier.

His face seized with an agonizing cry. He glanced around for the perpetrator, sighting his prayer book lying face down— its pages sprawling and singed, its cover blackened from the hateful fire. Next to it lay his red prayer pillow given to him by his dead father, sooty and singed as well. His mind froze at the sight of the sacred items that had guided his morning ritual, compounded by the pain lancing up his leg.

A cry up ahead jolted Alexander from his mind freeze, beckoning him to rise and follow the siren call toward the front of the great hall. He hobbled across the bruised and broken floor, pushing through the short hallway filled with rubble on toward the nave. Reaching the sacred space, he could tell the explosions had cascaded in a series of blasts from the back toward the front of the great, ancient room that had borne witness to thousands of homilies, prayers, and Eucharistic moments over the past millennia. The heat was intense, but the flames were less severe now, a geyser of water beginning to offer a miraculous balm for the forces of darkness that sought to consume the sacred space in the fires of hell. A pipe must have burst from the blasts.

But then a smoldering, gaping maw caught his attention sitting at the front where the altar containing the holy communion elements would have resided—perhaps an alternative detonation device had been planted at the high altar, making the image that much more ghastly knowing it had swallowed the memory-markers of Christ's sacrifice whole. Or had blown the bread and wine to bits. Either way, the image was dark, demonic. The altar where Zakaria would have been standing lay blown in jigsaw-puzzle chunks several feet away, as if the bomb blew it outward from its intended target, the Body and Blood of Christ. Alexander's gaze darted frantically around in search of his beloved assistant.

He heard a moan a few feet away down the center aisle. A pile of disfigured wooden pews sat strewn about like a pile of toothpicks blown apart by a playful little boy. The sight seized his breath and squeezed his stomach.

The bottom half of Zakaria had been blown with jagged indifference at the waist. A few feet away, his legs dangled down into the gaping mouth of hell that had opened where he had stood declaring the love of Christ and preparing the memory-markers that bore witness to that love. His intestines were spilling out of his body like a mangled mess of slippery, swollen sausages vying for some semblance of order. When he saw Alexander staring at him a few feet away with wide-eyed shock, his lips curled into a slight smile, eyes focusing in delight.

"Father..." Zakaria gasped, motioning Alexander to his side in a flipping gesture with his one free hand. The other arm lay pinned under a larger piece of the ceiling that had cracked down from the heavens.

Sour, metallic liquid began working its way up from the core of Alexander's belly. He swallowed hard, suppressing his body's visceral reaction to the gore that lay before him. He hurried to his friend who lay dying, slipping on a pool of blood that had spilled out from Zakaria's open cavity, nearly sending him back down on his wounded right leg.

He caught himself on the remains of a wooden pew and dropped down to comfort his friend. "Brother Zakaria," he said in breathless whimpers, "I am so sorry! I am so sorry I left you here all alone. I should have returned sooner..."

"Shh," Zakaria managed, wheezing in and out a shallow breath as water began streaming across the floor and the fires of hell hissed in protest. "Father, it's OK. It's OK. It's my time, Father. It's my time." The man was clearly struggling to get air, gurgling when he inhaled, a trickle of blood coming up when he exhaled.

Alexander tried to offer a word of comfort, a prayer or verse of Scripture, but his mouth just bobbed up and down uselessly. He couldn't think, he couldn't speak, he couldn't move. His mind was frozen in a blank cycle on repeat trying to process the carnage that had befallen his parish, his partner in ministry. He finally managed to reach down and cradle Zakaria's head, knowing the end was near.

"Read to me, Father," Zakaria whispered. "Read to me Scripture."

The last thing Alexander wanted to do was turn to the writings of the God who had failed to stop this mayhem from being unleashed against his people. But he complied, reciting the only Scripture that he could muster from memory for this moment of chaos.

"*'The Lord is my shepherd,'*" Alexander began, "*'I lack nothing. He makes me lie down in green pastures, he leads me beside quiet waters, he refreshes my soul.'*"

Part of the ceiling at the front tore off and crashed to the floor with a deafening boom, sending sparks flying high into the open ceiling and dusk sky.

Alexander shuddered from the sudden crash, as well as the chill of the water soaking his pants. But he continued, "*'He guides me along the right paths for his name's sake. Even though I walk through the darkest valley, I will fear no evil, for you are with me; your rod and your staff, they comfort me.'"*

From behind, more screams rang out, echoing around the hollowed-out shell of what used to be Alexander's pride and joy. Some were cries for help; others were cries for the dead.

Alexander continued his dirge: *"'You prepare a table before me in the presence of my enemies. You anoint my head with oil; my cup overflows. Surely your goodness and love will follow me all the days of my life, and I will dwell in the house of the Lord forever.'"*

Zakaria managed a satiated grin, mouthing a soundless *Amen* before his head lolled to the side and mouth went slack.

After he had finished reciting King David's beloved psalm of lamentation, Alexander continued staring forward, not willing himself to face what he knew to be true: The angels had carried his ministry partner out from the threshold of Hades and onto the gates of Heaven, right into the arms of his loving Savior.

Tears streamed down his face as he sank to the desecrated floor, cradling Zakaria and weeping over his loss. Several firefighters streamed past him to attend to the hellish scene trying to rise back up around the young priest. A few of them grabbed Alexander by the arms to hoist him out from the furnace of death even as their colleagues tried to extinguish what remained of it. But he wouldn't budge, wouldn't let go of his friend.

One of the men knelt down, looking at Alexander in his swollen eyes and consoling him while gently prying the mangled body of Zakaria out from his clenched arms.

The priest finally relented, collapsing into an emotional heap at the feet of his rescuer. Two of them held Alexander by his arms and rushed him out of the fragile husk of his parish.

Trailing him was the other firefighter cradling what was left of the husk of his friend and colleague in ministry.

When they reached the outside world, a huddled mass of Alexander's parishioners rushed him in a frenzy of delight and despair, both comforting him and seeking to be comforted. Through moist, blood-shot eyes, he stared at their faces in vague remembrance. He looked past them toward his smoldering parish only to panic with amnesic hysteria at the absence of Zakaria.

"Zakaria!" he shouted to a group of rescue workers. "My assistant is in there. He was leading the evening Mass in my absence. We need to get him out!"

One of the men came over to him, face confused and searching for a way to break the news he already knew.

And then he remembered, the shock giving way to hysterical sadness. He collapsed again, his body overtaken by violent, mournful cries.

His people crowded around him, embracing their beloved pastor and themselves, praying for him and their dead. Praying for the terrorists, their enemies, whom Jesus said to bless, not curse.

But everything within Alexander wanted to rise up with righteous, holy vengeance and slaughter those who had waged war against not only Ichthus, but his parish church.

Now it was personal.

CHAPTER 3

IT SEEMED like half the city was huddled around the broken body of Alexander's hollowed-out parish, its carcass looking like a charred jackal picked clean by scavangerous buzzards. They kept their distance as firefighters continued working to save what remained of the ancient building that had cradled Christianity for centuries. Yellow caution tape warned people to keep their distance from the fragile structure that would most likely be condemned and leveled.

While the spectacle continued outside, the cacophony of firefighting and the red-and-white strobe lights of rescue crafts flickering softly through his windows, Alexander lay resting in his parish quarters, thankful for the only respite still standing from the damnable day. His home AI assistant Barnabas had put on a playlist of jazz fusion from Europa, a calming balm for the man's troubled soul.

Members of his church council had insisted on keeping him company and tending to his wounds, but he sent them away, insisting he was fine. He wanted to be alone to process what had happened to his precious parish. He wanted to let himself sob in the silence of the night at the loss of so much life—and shake his fist at the good Lord above for letting it happen.

He was told fifty-three of his parishioners had died, nearly twenty of them children. One of them Zakaria. Nearly half of his church had been taken out by the coordinated bomb blasts, along with most of his church building. The rest of the injured were mending in hospital beds in town, some for weeks. The ancient structure that had stood the test of centuries, armies, and heresies had been decimated in one fell swoop.

Alexander held an ice pack to his head and nursed a tumbler of scotch, a balm for the inconceivable turn of events. His head still throbbed from the explosion and body ached from the beating he had taken, but it was more than that. A question jabbed at his brain like an icepick, the only one that mattered to him:

Who the hell was responsible for unleashing the fires of Hades upon his people?

For weeks, there had been rumors of such terror rumbling toward his hometown after several churches had been decimated by similar acts of evil. But nothing had come of them.

Then his mind leaped to the hooded figure darting down the pathway from his parish grounds and plowing into him on his ascent.

Was that the perpetrator? The tattoo he had glimpsed blazed into his mind's eye, a familiar marking that begged for a revelation. Two intersecting lines bent at either end. Perhaps it was a clue into the identity of similar bombings the past several months, the ones that had been marching across Alkebulana and on toward Tripolitania—and right to the threshold of his parish.

Alexander moaned in tune with a searing pain that arched through his head as he tried to unravel the mysterious, mayhemic events.

As he lay rubbing his throbbing head, he wondered about the future of his church. Where would they meet? How would they rebuild their already small community out of the traumatic rubble? Would they even want to rebuild in light of the ever-present threat of death and persecution increasingly raising its fanged head across the Republic? Within moments, his ministry had collapsed in a heaping mound of bodies and bricks. His eyes began to moisten thinking about the loss of life, the bodies of entire families and of children bloodied and broken amidst the twisted metal and chunks of concrete.

And then there was the future of the worldwide Church. She had survived Time's tests a thousand-fold. She'd survived intellectual attacks from Greek philosophy, modern rationalism, postmodern deconstructionism, and now ultramodernism's hyper-pluralism. She'd survived nationalistic attacks by the Roman Empire, Muslim invaders during the Middle Ages, and totalitarian persecutors during the twentieth and twenty-first centuries of the Information Age. She had survived threats from within that almost dismantled her, threats from schisms and alternative, false teachings. Through it all, Ichthus survived, and with scars to prove it.

But the present darkness of the *Homo Deus* Age was a different story—the age of the God-Man. Sure, the Reckoning had offered a measure of toleration across Solterra, but the advent of the alt-spiritual movement Panligo heightened the prolonged purpose-driven effort to stamp out the Church from the face of the planet once and for all. And led by Christian leaders, no less, representing the spectrum of Ichthus sects. It was not surprising Cardinal Weiss and Apollos Nicolai from the Protestant Orthodoxy wing of the Church led the way. That standard bearer of theological compromise had left behind the fundamental tenets of historic Christianity centuries ago. But Father Josiah Abasi's departure, a champion of Evangelical Orthodoxy, was shocking. The fallout was certain, and it would be severe.

Alexander eased himself forward and took a swig of his scotch, the smoky, spicy liquid hitting his stomach hard. He sighed with numbed pleasure then sank back into his sofa. His mind drifted back to the Church, wondering about the average Christian who was already holding on to their faith by a camel's hair width. How would Panligo affect their faith, the next generation's faith who composed a slim minority anyway within the Republic?

Chirp-chirp, a tone sounded forth, breaking his concentration. *Chirp-chirp*.

He glanced at his mobile device resting on the floor beside him. The sleek sapphire surface pulsing with an impatient-looking cardinal. Father James Ferraro.

One end of Alexander's mouth curled upward with no small amount of joy at seeing his mentor. He must have heard the news.

He picked up the device and answered the call. "Hey, Padre."

"Praise God from whom all blessings flow! You're alive, my son! I just received the news. Horrible, horrifying news."

Alexander took in a breath and rubbed his face with his weary palm, then sighed. "I'm still reeling myself, Father. Numb, really. Completely disbelieving the truth of it all. And I was there to witness it firsthand."

"Zakaria...How is he?"

His throat caught with emotion; an agonizing sting rose to his eyes. "He is in the arms of his Savior now."

There was an audible sigh. "Did you see him? Was he in pain?"

Alexander paused, measuring his words. "I was there with him when he passed, yes. He died..." He went silent, his mind's eye flooding with the sight of the man lying in a pool of blood and intestines. He settled on: "peacefully."

"Thank the Lord," Father Jim whispered.

A long silence rested between the two men.

"Any further word about Father Abasi?" Alexander asked, trying to move the conversation out of the realm of his devastation.

"Yes, I'm afraid. He was spotted by our operatives in Berlin arriving at the cathedral of Cardinal Weiss."

The mention of Dominic's name along with Josiah made Alexander's stomach clench with dread. It was as if he had suffered two deaths: the death of his church to terrorists and the death of his ministry colleague to a heretic. He wanted to retch; he thought he might.

He sighed and clenched his jaw, then said through gritted teeth, "I'm in, Father."

"What's that, lad?"

"In this fight for the faith. I'm in."

He was met with a sigh, perhaps in relief. "Good, my boy. Because Patmos was only the beginning."

"Only the beginning?" Alexander said sitting up, his knee lancing with pain. "What do you mean?"

"Your little trip back in time, riding the space-time continuum in all of its sci-fi glory, retrieved exactly what we needed. The multimedia experience of the sights and sounds from the apostle John are breathtaking. But it's not enough; we need more."

"I don't understand, Padre. Shouldn't his live testimony work wonders?"

Father Jim explained, "When the apostle John died in AD 100, there was a massive shift in the Church from what we call the apostolic era to the post-apostolic era. When he was alive, and there was a theological or ecclesiological controversy, the various regional leaders could appeal to the apostles, specifically John before his death. He was the lynchpin that held

Ichthus together as she grew and progressed. But after he died, there was no one left. There was no book stamped 'Holy Bible, NIV 2078 edition' early Christians could just turn to during times of persecution and controversy, like we can now. So the bishops responded to critics both inside and outside the Church by remembering what the apostles had taught, then gathering, preserving, and interpreting their writings. And then the long process began of hammering, honing, and hardening the teachings of the Church based on the teachings of Jesus Christ and preserved and explained by his apostles."

"Padre," Alexander moaned, lying back down again. "Thanks for the impromptu lecture, but where's this going? My head is already throbbing from the beating I took."

"Sorry, my boy. What I'm getting at is, we need to retrieve that record. We need to recapture how the historic faith developed over the centuries because our world is losing that faith. Especially since Panligo is stepping up its efforts to dismantle and discredit the Church as we know it. And I'm afraid the attack on your parish portends something as wicked rising up on the not-too-distant horizon."

"What now," Alexander said with a hint of complaint. "I can't take much more of this."

Father Jim hesitated. He cleared his throat and said, "I'm afraid it's your friend, Father Abasi. In the hours since you left Kiev, he has circulated a letter amongst the Ministerium members making a personal appeal on behalf of Cardinal Weiss and Father Nicolai. It is an impassioned appeal to our fellow priests and priestesses, speaking about his own conversion to the cause and theological necessity of recognizing God in the other religious faiths, especially the saving movement of God amongst religious bodies outside the Church. Apparently, forgetting Saint Augustine's *extra Ecclesiam nulla salus*."

"There is no salvation outside the Church," Alexander said.

"Impressive. You've remembered your Latin."

"I had an impressive teacher."

Father Jim chuckled. "At any rate, it's really quite dreadful. I'm afraid we are entering a new crusade of sorts in order to contend for the faith once for all entrusted to Christ's saints. And you're leading the charge, Alexander. You and Sasha. Do it for Father Abasi and the people his rising apostasy will impact." He paused before adding: "Do it for Zakaria."

The mention of those names twisted in Alexander's belly, sour names for different reasons. But Father Jim was right. The attack on his parish activated something within him that longed for vengeance. He wanted to avenge his friend's death, and all the other men, women, and children who had been under his care and protection. He also wanted to slap that smug grin off from Apollos's face.

But who the heck was he, anyway? Just some small-town priest of a burned-down parish who secretly harbored his own doubts about the teachings that sat at the heart of Ichthus, that's who. He had begun to wonder whether he had made the biggest mistake of his life following his dead father into the priesthood—all while former classmates like Sasha Pavlovich put their stamp on the world by discovering time travel, of all things! And Father Jim was pleading with him to jump into the thick of it all? To save a faith that was fraying at the edges a little more with each passing week, fueled by the march of history and an increasingly intolerant Republic?

"I can hear hesitation in your voice, Father Zarruq, so let me remind you of something."

Alexander's neck warmed with the embarrassment of being caught with hesitancy. "And what is that?"

"Do you remember the words I spoke to you the day of your ordination to the office of the priesthood?"

He searched his memory, but came up empty, the ache from the evening needling his head again. "Sorry, no."

"Well, let me refresh you." Father Jim cleared his throat, then began to recite from memory: "My brother, as a priest, it will be your task to proclaim by word and deed the Gospel of Jesus Christ, and to fashion your life in accordance with its precepts. You are to love and serve the people amongst whom you work, caring alike for young and old, strong and weak, rich and poor. You are to preach, to declare God's forgiveness to penitent sinners, to pronounce God's blessing, to share in the administration of Holy Baptism and in the celebration of the mysteries of Christ's Body and Blood, and to perform the other ministrations entrusted to you. In all that you do, you are to nourish Christ's people from the riches of his grace and strengthen them to glorify God in this life and in the life to come."

Alexander smiled at the memory of that bright spring day in Britannia, kneeling on those cold, hard flagstones that made up the ancient chapel hall before his favorite professor who had become a second father to him. Although much of the province, like much of the rest of the Republic, had secularized centuries past, the Dominican friars of the former United Kingdom had kept the embers of Ichthus education burning bright and strong over the generations. And he had been the recipient of their deep learning and spiritual discipleship, preparing him for such a time as this.

He replied, "Yes, Padre, I do remember."

"And then you answered a series of questions, asking if you were ready to commit to the path of priesthood, do you remember that?"

Did he ever. He was a nervous wreck kneeling before the

crowded hall, and he had inadvertently answered in the negative when asked if he believed that he had been truly called by God. Sent the presiding bishop into a coughing spell at the mistake. But he recovered and enthusiastically affirmed his calling to shepherd Christ's flock.

"Yes, I do," Alexander said.

Father Jim continued, "And one of those questions was whether you would undertake being a faithful pastor to all whom you are called to serve, laboring together with them and with your fellow ministers to build up the family of God, correct?"

"I remember that. But, I'm sorry, what are you saying?"

"What I'm saying is, you no longer have a parish. I'm sorry, but it's true. Not only because of the dastardly, Satanic designs last evening, but because the worldwide Church needs you, Alex. And given your connections with our time-travel discovering Sasha and the fruits of your past labor on that front, it seems as though you have been plucked from the pastures by the Great Shepherd himself for a new mission. One in service of his flock scattered across the Republic. So will you labor together with those whom you have been called to serve and along with all else in the Ministerium to build up the family of God, knowing that Christ has sent you forth in all authority and is standing alongside you unto the ends of the Earth—even unto the ends of time itself?"

Alexander went silent at the thought that he had been chosen by Jesus himself to man this mission of retrieval. He wasn't sure about that—truth be told, he thought the notion utterly absurd. He doubted very much that Jesus had fingered him for some divine task of ecclesial import. But whatever. He had to hand it to the man: Father Jim could certainly be persuasive when called to the task.

He shook his head and sighed. "What would you have me do, Padre?"

"The Fidelium is gathering again on the morrow. Come, and prepare to fight with every single weapon from the Lord's armory at our disposal."

Alexander's stomach dropped beneath his sofa at the thought of yet another clandestine ecclesial mission. His mouth watered for another ribbon of those synthetic narcotics he had come to both despise and depend upon—the minty goodness melting against his tongue and feeding him the peace that would soothe his synapses firing on all cylinders. On the street, the thin narcowafers that went for a few Republic *merca* credits a pop had been crudely nicknamed "hosts," after the thin unleavened wafers that served as the memory-marker of Christ's Body, broken on the cross for the sins of the world.

He cursed himself for his weakness, not to mention his seeming sacrilege, but he didn't care. He needed his fix if he was going to do what Father Jim was asking of him again.

He took a breath, then said, "Alright, Padre. You win. Nicaea here I come."

Dᴏᴍɪɴɪᴄ Wᴇɪss sᴛᴏᴏᴅ at the high altar beneath a golden crucifix suspended from the ceiling of wood and steel working out a wicked wrinkle from the black cassock that gave him the right to stand there in the first place. A candelabra of twelve candles, one for each of Jesus' disciples, wicks burning with bright clarity, and a bank of prayer candles flanked him on either side lit by the expectant faithful offered the only light that evening. Which is how the man preferred it.

Darkness punctuated by light struggling for a hearing.

The vestments, edged by crimson piping and reaching to the floor, had been handed down to him by his father upon ordination, the one who had presided over the sacred space for nearly his entire life. And that ministerial cloak had come to him by his own father and his father before him, men who had preached impassioned homilies directing their congregations toward the divine and led weekly Mass to nourish and ground their flock's faith. It had been this way stretching back generations. The priesthood was a family gig.

"These blasted garments..." he cursed, the candles offering just enough light to show angular folds in the polyester fibers. "You'd think with all of our progress over the centuries, Ichthus would be able to put together a proper vestment that kept its form."

He wrinkled his brow with irritated concentration and massaged his thumb against the fabric, his mind tweaked with a compulsive obsession that demanded order. As he continued rubbing out the wrinkle, waiting for his guest to arrive, he caught sight of himself in a gilded ancient column that had been polished to perfection—the sacred candlelight causing his reflection to glint off the surface and his sinful heart to take in the view with vain appreciation.

He eyed himself, his face brightening at the sight of his milky skin and perfectly coiffed hair drained of pigmentation, his well-apportioned nose flanked by high cheekbones and eyes of ice edged by white brows above.

'*My guardian angel,*' his mother would coo when he was younger, trying to infuse his bleached complexion with a specialness, a sacredness in light of the world's mockery and taunts. The one who had raised him, that is.

Weiss. White. Indeed he was, having been born with albinism, a stain in the gene pool of humanity that was all at once tolerated and reviled in Solterra by both the Republic and polis alike.

He had always thought his surname a fitting one, a sign of having been elected by Christ himself for his chosen, predestined purpose. But then he learned the truth of the matter: He had been discarded as an infant in an abandoned village somewhere in Europa still humming with toxins from the fallout in the wars leading up to the Reckoning, the ancient practice of exposure having received a renaissance in the ultramodern world. Perhaps it was an inevitable, logical extension of the abortive practices made legal in the twentieth century. More likely, with overpopulation a perennial, worldwide concern, some regions of the Republic increasingly employed more extreme measures to limit the human race. A practice Solterra had turned a blind eye to with disinterest.

Fortunately for him, he was rescued by a kind, infertile middle-aged couple who had been part of a resistant movement within the Republic against the barbaric practice. Just as Christians had before during the time of Rome, caring for infants abandoned to the unforgiving elements and wild beasts of the wilderness, dying from exposure to the bite of the bitter cold or roaming wolves. Had it not been for them adopting him as their own, he would have boiled in the cauldron of excessive, climatic heat and leftover toxins. Or perhaps been ripped limb-from-limb by the rabid beasts roaming such abandoned sites of Europa. He shuddered at the truth of his story, struck by the word that saved his life—in more ways than one.

Adoption.

Dominic glanced at the cross hovering above him, recalling a passage from the Holy Scriptures of Ichthus that had meant the world to him and his faith because of his parents' one, small, heroic act, the first chapter of Saint Paul's letter to the Ephesians:

> *Praise be to the God and Father of our Lord*
> *Jesus Christ, who has blessed us in the heav-*
> *enly realms with every spiritual blessing in*
> *Christ. For he chose us in him before the*
> *creation of the world to be holy and blame-*
> *less in his sight. In love he predestined us for*
> *adoption to sonship through Jesus Christ, in*
> *accordance with his pleasure and will—to*
> *the praise of his glorious grace, which he has*
> *freely given us in the One he loves.*

Chosen, predestined, adopted.

He caught sight of his lily-white skin and straw hair again in the gilded column, those same childhood feelings of being chosen a Weiss—predestined a *weiss*, a person of white—rising to the surface. All because he was adopted by two followers of a prophet from Nazareth who died, then was reported to have risen back to life, and whose memory lived on in and through the lives of his disciples—those disciples, *Vater* and *Mutter*.

He smiled to himself at the memory of his parents, dead for nearly a decade now, a sweet memory to be sure. He wondered what his priest father would think about his change of course.

He startled at the rattling of a door at the far end of the nave. It swung on squeaky hinges before banging against the old, cold stones of the cathedral.

Right on time.

He could hear someone shuffling through the darkened space, his footfalls fast approaching. Soon, a man robed in the same black cassock emerged into the candlelight, eyes white with apprehension set against a dark face a world away from his own.

Yes, I imagine you are quaking in those vestments of yours, given what you're about to do...

Dominic stepped down the marble stairs and met the man in front of the high altar. "Josiah, how is life in Kinshasa these days?" he asked, extending his hand and outstretching his other arm for an embrace.

Bishop Abasi grasped it and obliged his welcome. "Cardinal Weiss," he said, "Things are exceedingly delicate, as you can imagine."

"Yes, I imagine they are. All the better of you to meet me here."

Abasi glanced over Dominic's shoulder, then back behind him and around the space. "Where is Nicolai?"

"On his way."

The man nodded. "And the woman?"

"Elsewhere."

A silence fell between the men. The quiet, almost holy hum of the atmospheric HVAC controls preserving the ancient space, offered the only soundtrack for the hour leading up to the moment when they advanced their work to the next blessed level.

"A bit ironic, isn't it?" Abasi said, wringing his hands together and taking in the sight that soared heavenward in the faint candles' glow.

"What's ironic?"

The man furrowed his brow and stared at Dominic a beat. "That we're standing in the place made famous by that Germanian just over seven hundred years ago."

"Ah, yes. Martin Luther. The rogue monk who sought to reform Ichthus those centuries ago. Little did he know his little list of ninety-five ecclesial demands would be the spark that lit the fuse to blow the Church to pieces."

Father Abasi licked his lips and started wringing his hands again, eyeing the place with a look that concerned Dominic. Was it apprehension he saw? Perhaps he was having second thoughts.

Something he could not let happen.

He grasped Father Abasi's shoulders, startling the man. "Are you ready for your own pyrotechnics, Josiah?"

The Alkebulanan bishop hesitated.

"Because there's no going back once you light your own fuse. You heard what happened at the conclave. Cardinal Ferraro will not stop until he personally hunts down every last man or woman he deems a heretic and burns them at the stake."

The man took a breath, then dropped his hands, raised his

head, and stiffened. He nodded. "I am. For Ichthus, for humanity."

Excellent...

A smile crept across Dominic's mouth. His eyes narrowed and he dipped his head slightly with the pleasure of knowing what it meant that one of the most powerful bishops in Alkebulana—not to mention conservative Evangelical Orthodoxy—was defecting to Panligo.

Ichthus would explode once again.

This time for good.

CHAPTER 5

THE DEEP SUBMERGENCE vehicle docked at the seaport in Byzantium none too soon for Alexander's liking. He hated travel of any sort, especially the kind that zipped beneath the Mediterranean Sea.

In many ways, he didn't know which was worse: the old pre-Reckoning air travel that was banned—whether from climactic climate change or Solterra's totalitarian control, it wasn't clear—hurtling through the atmosphere in an aluminum tube thousands of feet above ground; or the kind of titanium tubes he was stepping out of that had just hurtled through thousands of pounds of water hundreds of feet below sea level. Most of the journey was spent running through a hundred scenarios that could befall them along the way. None of them good, and all of them resulting in a shared locker with Davy Jones and the rest of the sailors of yore rotting at the bottom of the sea.

He slipped a narcowafer on his tongue and pressed it against the roof of his mouth, his head instantly swimming with relief from the anxiety of the travel compounded by his clandestine mission back to where he hoped he'd never again have to travel. He closed his eyes as he continued shuffling through the queue of passengers—

Then ran into the back of a very large man with a buzzed head and smelling of salted beef, wearing tight black pants and a white t-shirt cut off at his midsection, a trend that had run its course last century but apparently continued on through the incarnation before him.

The hulking man spun around, his neck sagging under the weight of way too many kabobs, ears sagging under the weight of even more silver rings. His eyes took Alexander in, then narrowed. He let out a huff through a bulbous nose that began to flare, like a bull catching sight of a crimson España cape and ready to charge.

"Watch it, *mystik*," the man growled, a term of derision that instantly spelled trouble for Alexander.

He stepped back with caution. The bull stepped forward, his arms rippling with cords of muscle beneath his sun-bronzed skin billowing beneath his cutoff t-shirt.

"Forgive me," Alexander stammered, lowering his head and raising an arm in apology. He took another step back, self-consciously grabbing the white collar that ringed his neck.

Passengers tried sidestepping around the pair, but the traffic jam worsened behind their roadblock. Someone shouted a curse a few yards back. Another man echoed his complaint and shouted for them to get a move on in a tongue Alexander didn't recognize.

The bull growled again, repeating his *mystik* curse and adding a few more choice words.

Then one more: *sanguinazi.*

Alexander sucked in a breath at the word. The word to end all words. The highest insult to those who claimed allegiance to the faith of Ichthus.

Stretching back before even the Reckoning, the term of

derision began popping up on the pre-DiviNet Internet before making its way into the mainstream. It was a way to mock those who claimed the name of Christ as 'blood-eaters' who practiced superstitious ways and bigots who believed regressive ideologies harmful to the Republic.

His heart was hammering in his head now, the word ricocheting around his consciousness and igniting a rising fear at what the man might do to him at uttering such a hateful word.

All at once, the man spit to the ground and hefted his body back around. Then he continued lumbering through the terminal, disappearing through the throngs of people.

Alexander stood still. He swallowed hard and took a few stabilizing breaths at the altercation as people streamed around him.

That was a close one.

Wiping several beads of sweat that had trailed down the sides of his forehead, he took a hesitant step forward but faltered after someone else in a rush nearly sent him stumbling to the ground. He recovered, then joined the crowd of travelers trying to catch their connection, blending in and trying not to draw any more attention to himself—given where he was going and what he was doing, and the discrimination he had just experienced.

Ever since the Reckoning and the establishment of Solterra —the republic of assembled nation-states cobbled together and brokered in the aftermath from the disasters of climate change that had ravaged the world and fallout from decades of civil wars and conflict—life as a follower of Jesus Christ had become tenuous. It's why the religion had become designated as *Ichthus* at the turn of the century, a throwback to the ancient symbol of the earliest Christians when it was struggling under the weight of Empire Rome.

The word had become a derogatory curse across the world

the past few decades as Christian brothers and sisters were forced to resurrect the symbol through the superheated fires of persecution through much of sub-Saharan Alkebulana; across all of Asiatica; in parts of Americana, Noramericana, Louisiana, Cascadia, and California; and even in Mexicana—just as the earliest Christians themselves had created the symbolic word in the first place during imperial persecution throughout the Roman Empire.

The early Church had identified friend from foe using two simple arcing lines that intersected at one end, mirroring one another to form a fish. In later centuries, *ichthus*, the Greek word for the aquatic being, became known as the "Jesus fish." Since the Reckoning, it had been adopted as a banner of pride to separate the remnant of Christianity from the rest of the world religions by adopting the culture's curse and re-identifying with its central figure and beliefs formed as an acrostic with its letters: *Jesus* (I) *the anointed Christ* (Ch), *Son* (U) of *God* (Th), *our Savior* (S).

Ichthus.

It was this symbol that had become a curse on the lips of much of the Republic. Not as bad as *sanguinazi*, but still an insult. For though the world knew the name of Jesus, they neither honored nor thanked him. And they certainly didn't honor or thank the bearers of that name. Some of that was the fault of Christians themselves; the Church certainly had a way of turning people off to Jesus with masterful strokes. But it was also the fault of the world, who refused to have ears to listen and eyes to see what Jesus Christ himself wanted to tell the world through his followers, his ambassadors bearing witness to the truth of repentance from rebellion against God and rescue from sin and death through Jesus alone. Jesus Christ himself, the Son of God our savior, said it best: *'Everyone will hate you because of me.'*

And hate they did, spitting *Ichthus* out at the sheep of Christ like venom, doing their damnedest to bar them from participating in the Republic, even slaughtering them with indifferent abandon in certain sectors. But the Church eventually wore it like a badge of honor, for the rest of what Jesus said mattered as much as the truth of the first part: *'the one who stands firm to the end will be saved.'*

But where the average Christian could blend in and adapt to the culture, though still exiled within it and threatened with persecution—it was an entirely different story for the caretakers of the Church, the Ministerium. There was once a time in the not too distant past when ministers and priests were a respected professional field. Right up there with doctor and lawyer. Well, maybe not lawyers, but still. However, the Zeitgeist, the Spirit of the Age, has a way of poisoning the well—and boy did it poison.

Hence *mystik*, a curse word among the ultramodern citizens of the Republic for priests of the Church. People began to see them as peddlers of a dangerous breed of superstitious, regressive ideology in a world ruled by technological advancement and social progress. While tolerated by the Republic in theory, Ichthus had it bad among the actual citizens of the assembly of nations. Some parts were safer than others, like Noramericana, forged out of the Old South of the splintered former U.S.A., and some of the regions in Alkebulana, Alexander's own home of Tripolitania being one of them. Given the hostilities, especially against members of the Ministerium, he rarely traveled dressed as a priest. In the weariness from his parish bombing he had forgotten to change. And nearly paid the price for it.

He prayed to the good Lord above that the altercation didn't portend wicked things to come for the rest of his journey.

He made it through security without so much as a passing

glance from the AI humanoid, the narcowafer doing wonders for his nerves. He joined his fellow travelers and began the ascent to the surface above, blue light filtering down through a glass enclosure holding the sea water at bay and casting undulating ripples and crisscross patterns of azure and indigo over the travelers.

A weak smile played across Alexander's face as he continued his ascent, recalling his clandestine mission to reach the gathered faith-keepers at the conclave of the Fidelium just a week ago. He wondered how Tara Rodriguez was faring, his Ministerium special-ops chaperone who had given him a run for his money. His pulse quickened thinking about her close-cropped jet-black hair and well-fitting clothes.

It had been at least a century since priests were allowed to marry, both men and women members of the Ministerium. He had dated a few fine Alkebulana women over the years, as well as a couple of students from his years studying at Oxford, but he had never made much progress on that front. He had resigned himself to a life of celibacy, married to the Bride of Christ instead. However, perhaps the mysterious Ministerium woman could change his lot in life.

Alexander followed the flow of humans and humanoids out from the cool, sanitized seaport of clean lines and pallet of ocean colors and out into stifling, sweaty Byzantium, the regional capital of Arabia-Persia at the center of the reconstituted ancient empires under the terms of the Reckoning. Temperatures had to be in the low hundreds, compounded by the suffocating humidity made that much more unbearable by the stench of rotting fish and garbage wafting in from the sea and some ungodly part of the city. Solterra liked to style itself as a utopian paradise, where everything was in unified order and done '*For Humanity!*' as its citizens were programmed to intone. But most people knew better. Pax Solterra of the singular, united Earth may well indeed reign from sea to shining sea; that he'd give the Republic credit for. But much of the world seemed no better off than the days of the Roman Empire from two millennia ago.

He breathed through his mouth, shielding his nose with his arm of white linen vestments, and made for the terminal pick-up zone. A mishmash of soaring ultramodern buildings of gleaming glass and titanium and ancient few-story ones of stone and steel greeted Alexander as he hustled toward a vacant cab hovering at the front of a queue of magnacars.

Laughter and a few high-pitched whistles up ahead drew his attention as he made his way to the vehicle. A band of men, hooting and hollering and whistling, surrounded a platform off to the side outside the terminal.

On top was someone who looked like they were doing some sort of performance for the crowd.

They were thin, not more than five feet tall. Shirtless, skin bronzed and ribs jutting out at ungodly angles. Hair died bright pink and cropped to the chin, with long, black eyelashes and cheeks blushed to perfection. A matching pink tutu fluffed in the faces of the onlookers as the figure twirled around a chrome pole on top a platform with multi-colored lights flickering in the closing evening light.

Another round of cheers arose from the crowd, one eager man groping for the body of the dancer and finding some success—her face registering sheer horror through a pained, painted performer's smile.

Alexander twisted his face with disgust at the misogynistic scene playing out in public. Other passengers were now coming in, seeking the woman for their own lustful look, but he'd had more than enough, wanting to burn his eyes with a blowtorch at the sight.

He went to pull away when the clarity of the matter suddenly hit him.

No, not a woman.

A child.

And a boy...

Maybe thirteen or fourteen. Spinning and grinding against the pole for the men as they threw cards of *merca* credits at his feet. Feigning delight and wonder, but looking scared out of his wits.

One of the men grabbed for the pink hair as the boy bent down to straddle the platform, taking it off and holding it above his head as a trophy. The boy's close-cropped black hair was now exposed, confirming the truth of what was happening.

He was an *Eromenos*. A beloved. Not necessarily a sex slave, but might as well have been. They were young boys dressed as girls and offered platforms—literally—to display their goods for the world to affirm and idolize and lust.

Alexander's chest grew tight and bowels went weak with the depravity of it all. He had heard about such blatant, open-air exhibitions of debauchery on display in cities throughout the Republic. For some ungodly reason, Solterra not only tolerated it but approved of it in the name of diversity and inclusion. But he had never believed it to be true.

Now he knew better.

Kyrie eleison...

Lord, have mercy.

On that boy. On the souls of those men.

On the soul of Solterra itself.

He peeled his gaze away from the dancer, a deep sadness welling up within, the imprint of the boy's pained expression searching for safety and relief etched on his mind's eye. He wiped his eyes and shuffled to a vacant magnataxi.

As he approached the cab that had seen better days, the up-door unfolded like one of those ancient DeLoreans he had obsessed over as a boy. He slid into the backseat that didn't fare much better than the outside, the scuffed blue upholstery and a strong whiff of something sour making him think twice about his choice.

"Where to?" a rather large humanoid grunted, a plebe as they were affectionately known among the human types for being of the lower-class AIs in the Republic.

"Iznik," Alexander said, the ultramodern town of the ancient one known by the Church as Nicaea.

The rotund AI humanoid twisted to face him in a herky-jerky movement. "You!" he grunted again with derision.

Alexander furrowed his brow as he stuffed his long, lanky legs in place, staring at the mechanical human that creepily seemed to recall who he was.

Then it hit him.

The gruff, grande plebe from his last mission with Tara racing to the conclave.

His face fell. He closed his eyes and sighed. *Of course...*

Last time, the AI put up a major fuss for the long drive to Iznik. Tara had to pay the plebe nearly a week's worth of digital *merca* credits.

This was not going to go well.

"Where's your master, little doggie?"

Little doggie. The insult the AI had lobbed at him the last time around.

"And this time you pay in full at the start!" the plebe yelled.

Yep. Not good at all.

"Fine. How much."

The humanoid held up ten fingers.

"Are you kidding me?!" Alexander jolted forward toward the humanoid. "A thousand *mercas*?"

The plebe smiled and offered a single nod.

He sat back in a huff, then reached for the door. "That's highway robbery. I don't have to take this."

"Suit yourself, doggie." It snorted, then added, "But good luck finding driver to take you to Iznik for less."

The plebe was right. He was stuck.

He sat back in a huff and raked a hand through his hair. "Fine. A thousand *mercas* it is." He whipped out his mobile, the face of the thin sapphire device asking for the Republic credits. He jammed *Accept* then stuffed it back in his pocket, cursing under his breath as his hard-earned money zipped across DiviNet from his account into the blasted plebe's.

The humanoid offered a growly chuckle before turning around and throwing the vehicle into gear. It lurched forward on a bed of air before drifting into the traffic exiting the seaport.

Alexander winced as he adjusted his position, trying to find comfort for his legs stuffed behind the gruff, grande plebe and settling in for the road ahead.

CHAPTER 6

NICAEA, ARABIA-PERSIA.

ALEXANDER SETTLED in and closed his eyes to avoid the plebe, but sleep was hard to come by with the cramped quarters and bumpy magnaroads filled with potholes and debris—which Solterra would surely deny, for it was all about the narrative of utopian order. Much easier to rewrite the truth of the problems in the backwoods corners of the Republic than confront the realities of life still plaguing Solterra. And potholes were the least of them.

'For Humanity!' was the rallying cry of the masses, conditioned by the Republic to believe the narrative written by those in power. Yeah, right. Food shortages and lack of clean water was still as much an issue in Solterra post-Reckoning. Same for the kind of meaningful employment that would provide for both. The rise of AI humanoids had taken most of the low-skill and even higher-skill jobs that people once worked. Though many were now under the employ of the Republic, others were left longing to live out their God-given identity as creators and workers. Which often flared tensions in parts of the Republic that were worse off than others.

But most people would rather believe the lie of peace and security than face the truth that things were not what the world had bargained for during the Reckoning and with the establishment of Solterra's charter—especially when they were fed their daily food rations (when it came), and given their allotment of housing and Republic-issued work assignment (when something opened), and the peace and security that had been so hard to come by for centuries finally arrived in a Solterra-issued gift box (when it was enforced).

He didn't know what to make of it all, and he certainly wasn't political. But often, it seemed like a situation of frogs boiling in a kettle, where one day the world would wake up to what it had done in the interest of peace and harmony and realize it was all an illusion. And too late to do anything about it.

The pair made it to Nicaea without a hitch in under two hours. Which was a blessedly good thing, because the sour stench seemed to grow with every passing kilometer. And eventually the packet of peanuts the Republic stewardesses so graciously handed out on the DSV for the trip across the Mediterranean would end up on the back of gruff, grande plebe very soon.

Which would open up a whole new set of problems.

The sun was quickly slipping beneath the horizon as the humanoid pulled up to a fountain dribbling dirty water at the center of town. Across the street, the same Coca-Cola sign next to a 7-11 that had greeted Alexander and Tara a week ago splashed crimson light across the darkening square. A few magnacars stood outside the modest convenience store that managed to survive the Republic's provisions and same-day deliveries. It seemed the human instinct to provide for oneself continued, especially when late-night snack runs were in order.

The plebe jolted to a halt, every one of Alexander's muscles and joints screaming in protest.

He thanked the AI, then promptly shoved through the

Alexander took a breath. "There was an...incident."

"An incident? Of what sort?"

"Totally my fault. Wasn't at all watching where I was going, and I accidentally bumped into a rather large bloke." He shook his head. "Which was not a good move."

"What did he do? Did he know who you were? Did he ask you anything?"

"No, I don't think so. But he did call me a *mystik*. Forgot to change my collar in the exhaustion and confusion from the night before."

Father Jim grunted. "Makes sense."

"There was something else."

He waited, then prodded, "Go on..."

"He also called me a—a *sanguinazi*."

"A *sanguinazi*, he said that?"

Alexander nodded. "Then he spat to the floor of the seaport. Thought he was going to string me up from the ceiling then and there. But he didn't. Just spat his insult and lumbered away."

"That is most concerning, the brazenness of the man calling you out as a member of Ichthus with such a slur. You're sure he walked off, that he didn't circle back to follow?"

"I'm sure."

"Because if he did—"

"He didn't. I'm sure of it."

Father Jim nodded and grunted again. "Let's just hope your little misadventure doesn't portend anything more for the journey ahead."

Soon a white, round church with a cross-shaped nave and elongated apse and crowned with a gleaming dome appeared. Church of Dormition dated from perhaps as early as the end of the 6th century. Destroyed in 1922, it was later restored to its original glory before the Reckoning using surviving walls. Back in the day, it was one of the most architecturally important Byzantine churches in Asia Minor and managed to remain one of the few churches to survive Muslim transformation. It was originally adorned with beautiful multicolored Byzantine mosaics from the 11th century. The restoration meticulously restored those original aesthetics while reinforcing it with ultramodern architecture.

The church gleamed in the full moonlight that rained down from the clear, cloudless night. It stood as a beacon of hope during these turbulent ecclesiastical times, a lighthouse guiding the arriving two members who had pledged themselves to not only teach the faith, but to keep and preserve it.

Father Jim drove around behind the church through a corridor of lush cypress trees, their canopy of leaves hiding the moonlight and concealing the entrance to a passageway that led deep underneath the church grounds. The car zoomed through the narrow entrance and slumped down into the passage, taking the passengers through a winding tunnel bathed in white light before arriving at a large car park where several similar vehicles were parked.

Alexander eased out of the magnacar. Father Jim did the same and motioned for him to follow. He led them toward a set of frosted double doors, their glass edged with chrome.

"Here we are," he said as the doors *whooshed* open. He headed down a hallway that transformed from the ultramodern architecture into an entirely different world.

Misshapen mud-colored brick stacked one on the other in awkward rows lined the walls. The spicy scent of aged earth tinged with the musty smell of a graveyard that bore memories from centuries past led them deep beneath the venerable church. Alexander recalled Father Jim explaining the first time he came how the Ministerium had the foresight to construct a separate chamber beneath the reconstructed church to provide secure accommodations for gatherings such as the conclave he had visited a week ago.

But he had no idea why he was being brought back there.

Father Jim turned the corner, leading them toward the chamber where the conclave was held, a sort of reconstructed Sistine Chapel after the seas rose and gobbled up Vatican City under its watery might. He could see the heavy wooden doors up ahead. They were closed and dark.

The cardinal stopped short at a door Alexander didn't recall seeing the last time he had been brought down the corridor.

Without a word, the man pressed a hand against a slab of glass to the right of what looked like a heavily reinforced door, complete with titanium ribbing. The kind you use when you want to keep the world out. For good.

Alexander looked on as the cardinal raised his head to a small, round camera above the glass scanner. A faint green beam of light shot out and scanned Father Jim's face, then *pinged* with recognition.

The door unlocked and retracted, revealing another world entirely different from that one.

"Into the looking glass we go, Alex," Father Jim said, motioning for Alexander to enter.

He took a hesitant step inside, mouth open and eyes taking in the unexpected scene.

Where they had been descending through a dimly lit hallway of stacked, baked bricks from centuries past, this one was bright with a gleaming whiteness from LED lights above lining walls of slate-gray concrete. It was empty, but for a few personnel hustling in and out of more doors of similar construction up ahead.

None of them looked like members of the Ministerium.

"What is this place?" Alexander asked, following Father Jim farther down the corridor.

"Why, the Ministerium, my boy." He glanced back at him with a wry grin.

"This is not the Ministerium I know. Nor is it the one we've been told about."

Father Jim chuckled. "Fair enough. It's the other side to the Ministerium coin, then."

Alexander went to offer a retort when another voice yelled out for Father Jim up ahead.

"Cardinal Ferraro," a man called.

Alexander didn't recognize the man. He was tall and of Anglo-Saxon descent by the looks of it, with close-cropped blond hair and wearing a charcoal uniform of some sort. Like one of those one-piece flight suits. Not the typical Ministerium member at all.

"Ah, just the man I wanted to see." Father Jim motioned for Alexander. "Alex, I'd like you to meet someone."

The man lumbered over with a swagger that exuded confidence. He was holding a knife and slicing into an apple. He popped a piece into his mouth, crunching on it with an echoey juiciness.

The man offered his hand to Alexander. "John Mark Ford. Pleased to meetcha."

He nodded and took it. "Alexander Zarruq."

He winced a little under the mystery man's vice-like grip. He liked to think he was in shape, but not like this guy. He clearly benched, keeping in tip-top shape. And apparently needed three names. Then there was that accent. Definitely not of this continent, but he couldn't place it. There was a twanginess to it that set his teeth on edge. And the knife sure was an unusual accessory. He looked like one of those GI-Joe collectible military action figures he had seen on DiviNet from back in the day. But that didn't make any sense.

"John Mark," Father Jim said, "came to us several months ago from the Republic Legion."

He glanced at the cardinal with a raised brow. "He's Solterra military?"

"Former," Ford said, slicing another piece of his apple with the long blade and popping it into his mouth.

The man didn't say much, either. Why the Ministerium was employing someone who defected from the Republic, and its military no less, made zero sense.

Father Jim nodded. "Indeed, he did. And just when Ichthus needed someone of his caliber and expertise. He's been working around the Ministerium the past few months, busying himself on a special project for the Fidelium and acting as head of operations."

"What special project?" Alexander asked.

The cardinal went to answer when a young deacon in a cassock a size too big ran up to Father Jim's side. He whispered something into his ear. The cardinal's face scrunched with irritation.

"What are you getting at, lad?" he said.

Looking embarrassed, the young man glanced at Alexander, then back to Father Jim.

"He's with me," the cardinal said.

"You should come have a look."

The deacon eased forward, glancing back and motioning for the group to follow.

Father Jim sighed and nodded, following the young man's lead. He brought them to another set of doors, went through the same routine as Father Jim at the one before, then ushered the group inside what looked to be a command center. The walls were lined with massive sapphire displays that resembled

Republic-issued broadcasters, all streaming various videos and other data. Men and women in similar uniforms as John Mark Ford were manning stations arrayed around the perimeter, monitoring the displays and pointing at tablets.

Alexander's breath quickened at the sight, for none of it looked like DiviNet. Which meant that this place was definitely not Solterra compliant, as all authorized information flowed through the Republic network.

This place was off the grid by a wide margin. He had never seen anything like it. He didn't even know such places existed anymore.

He flashed Father Jim a worried look as the man walked past him toward a raised dais that looked like a command post within what seemed like some sort of command center for Ichthus.

The deacon brought a large display to life at the center of one wall. Which sparked surprise and confusion amongst the trio.

The broadcaster gleamed with the image of Father Abasi. Standing next to him were two familiar men.

Alexander offered a gasp, echoed by the rumblings of several more around the room.

Father Jim leaned forward against a table on the dais, resting both fists on its surface, his face falling with dread, voicing what everyone else knew to be true.

"This shan't be good."

CHAPTER 7

"Greetings Ichthus, my fellow brothers and sisters in the faith."

The dark skin of the Bishop of Kinshasa was framed by the soft yellow light of candles bouncing off from a background of pale stone. He was seated behind the high altar in a cathedral of an unknown location upon red velvet-covered gilded chairs, flanked by two men.

Cardinal Dominic Weiss and Father Apollos Nicolai.

Alexander's pulse leaped forward at the sight of his university rival standing next to his missing friend. The sight of Cardinal Weiss didn't help matters either, the man who had infiltrated the conclave a week ago to offer a strong rebuttal to Father Jim after he and the other schismatic Christians had formed Panligo.

Whatever was about to go down...bad things were in store.

"Who is that fella?" Ford asked, popping the rest of his apple into his mouth and then crunching it to death.

"Josiah Abasi," Alexander said with a faltering voice, taking a step forward. "One of my best friends."

"And this is playing across DiviNet, throughout the Republic?" Father Jim asked with exasperation.

The deacon nodded grimly.

"I am Bishop Josiah Abasi, of Kinshasa," the man on the broadcaster said, "the central Alkebulanan province of Solterra. I have been a follower of Jesus Christ all of my life. However, it was only in the last decade that I dedicated myself as a servant of his Church, taking part in the Ministerium training and becoming a priest, and then becoming a bishop. Truth be told, I have always been more spiritual than religious," the man said with a chuckle, "not wanting to become entangled with the trappings of organized religion. Even before deciding to follow Jesus, I had understood that a ground of being exists that permeates all of life. I only stumbled into Ichthus after becoming fascinated with the person of Jesus, his love-filled teachings and sacrificial example of love. And becoming a priest within the Ministerium is a whole other story!" The man smiled broadly, his body lifting with another good-natured chuckle.

The corner of Alexander's mouth pulled into a smile at the sound of his laugh. He loved that laugh; he missed that laugh. It's what brought them together in the first place those years ago coming up through the Ministerium together. Abasi was the one he had leaned on when his father passed. The man had dropped everything to sit shiva with him through his time of mourning.

And there he was, sitting between Weiss and Nicolai. He felt his breath go out of him and stomach lurch forward with pained betrayal at what the man was doing, a sucker punch to the gut by the man who had been one of the truest friends he'd had.

Abasi continued, "So I have a significant past with Ichthus and with a commitment to the divine. Many of you watching have walked with me through my spiritual journey. We have done ministry together. Dreamed of new ways to connect people to the ground of their own being together in this ultra-modern world, rooted in the teachings of Jesus. Which is why I am now pleased to say that I have joined with the two men sitting next to me to lock arms with other like-minded individuals from similarly organized religious affairs to offer the world a united experience of the divine."

"This is unreal..." Father Jim said, coming up next to Alexander. He rested a knowing hand of solidarity upon his shoulder, saying nothing more but saying all he needed to say in the gesture.

Alexander turned to the man and swallowed. "Yes. It is."

"Let me begin with an ancient story," the bishop continued, "a parable about four blind men and a beast of unknown origin. As this story goes, one day a group of blind men heard that a strange animal had been brought into their village by a man traveling on his way through town, stabling him for the evening until the next day's journey. Out of curiosity, the men agreed that they must inspect and fully know what it was that the traveling man had brought into town—and by using the only means by which they could discern the foreign beast. By touch.

"So they sought out the traveling man and his mystery beast. When they found it, they groped about, feeling it in various ways and its various parts. You see, none of them on their own were aware of its shape and form in its entirety. Only in its divided particularity did each man conceive of the animal. So they agreed to reveal to each other what it was that they had discerned individually, understanding that their own perspective contributed to the whole constitution of the unknown beast.

"In the case of the first person, whose hand landed on the trunk, the man said, *'This being is like a thick snake.'* For another fellow, whose hand had grasped its ear, it seemed like a kind of fan, flapping this way and that. As for another person, whose hand was upon its leg, this one said, *'This here beast is a pillar, like that of a tree trunk.'* One fellow placed his hand upon the beast's side, describing it as a wall, immovable and impenetrable. Another, who felt its tail, described it as a rope. The last blind man felt its tusks and insisted, *'Surely the mystery is that which is hard and smooth, like a spear.'*

"So there we are: one man beheld the tail, another its tusks, then one more its trunk; one grasped the beast's ears, another touched its massive body, another its legs. When they reported back on what they had encountered, the report matched each of their personal experiences with the creature: it was hard or floppy, long or smooth, thick or immovable. Six different descriptions of the one elephant, coming from six different experiences."

Abasi took a breath, then grinned knowingly. "If you are as astute as I believe you are, brothers and sisters, you probably guessed the blind men were each describing different aspects of *Loxodonta*, the mighty elephant native to my home country of Alkebulana."

"Stuff and nonsense is what this is," Father Jim mumbled.

Alexander nodded in agreement. It was certainly a story he had heard before, a common refrain from the spiritual-but-not-religious crowd of the Republic who not only couldn't believe there was a God to begin with, but couldn't imagine there was only one *way* to God. They insisted there were multiple paths to the divine—multiple perspectives from all us blind men groping our way through our encounter with the elephant in the room. God, or the Divine, or the Universe, or whatever.

The bishop from Kinshasa leaned back and placed his hands on the altar in front of him. He continued, "You see, each of these men had a limited understanding of the singular elephant, didn't they? Each believed they understood the elephant completely based on their own personal experience—

even though that belief was based on a limited exposure. Because of their ignorance of the entire truth of the elephant, each of these blind men assumed the entire elephant matched their own limited description. And as the parable concludes, when they came together to describe and report on their revelation, not only did they disagree over the nature of that revelation, but they squabbled about it—declaring the other bearers of revelation about the elephant false and heretical and anathema.

"Of course, we enlightened ones know that an elephant isn't only tusks or legs like pillars. It isn't only a wiry tale or long trunk. It isn't just big flappy ears. And it isn't only a massive hard, rough wall-like body. No, the beast from my home country is composed of each characteristic described by the blind men. The elephant is the whole of their revelation."

The man chuckled and sat forward again. "So what on earth is the point of this story? Well, brothers and sisters of Ichthus, the moral of the parable is this: Each religion is like these blind men and our elephant is like the divine reality we understand to be God. Each religion has only a partial knowledge of the divine reality, only a limited experience and exposure to the ground of our being, the singular Absolute. Just like the six blind men in our story. We see that all religions are merely parts of the one divine whole—all describing the same elephant, the same Absolute, just in different ways.

"Which is why I am pleased to join with my brothers, here," Abasi said, motioning toward Cardinal Weiss and Father Nicolai on either side of him, "as well as other like-minded men and women throughout the Church. All in order to join hands with all the blind across the Republic, as it were, to offer a cohesive, unified assembly of spiritualists in search of the Spirit. From the Israelites to the Mohammedans, the Buddhists to the Hinduans, we've joined hands to welcome a new spiritual era of cooperation through Panligo."

The man swallowed and licked his lips, then glanced over to his right. "And now, I wish to turn it over to Cardinal Weiss."

Another camera angle dissolved into view, the man of white in a crimson cassock with gold piping coming into focus, his white face framed by hair of straw and eyes fixing the camera with an icy intensity.

"Thank you for your moving testimony, Bishop Abasi," Weiss started, the timbre of each word laced with the guttural intensity of old Germania. "And thank you for leading the charge to bring about a reformation within Ichthus in order to bring a spiritual awakening to Solterra. The primary core to this movement of the Spirit is the essential oneness of all beings, flowing from one single source. Saint Paul himself commended the ancient Athenians for their worship of the Unknown God, acknowledging *'For in him we live and move and have our being.'"*

"What the..." Father Jim exclaimed, taking an irritated step toward the display. He threw his arms into the air and complained, "The bloody fool is completely twisting Scripture! Absolutely mangling the Word of God to fit his fancy."

"And we are celebrating that oneness," the cardinal continued, "combining forces with the others who have intuited the Spirit in whom the whole of humanity lives and moves and has its being. The very nations and cultures of this great planet recognized this essential oneness and unity during the Reckoning, forming a united people through Solterra. Which, I must confess, is a bit embarrassing as a priest of Ichthus to realize culture had a clue before us Christians did. Although, I guess it is to be expected, given how often the Church has been on the wrong side of history, and how often culture has led Ichthus across the centuries."

He offered the camera a smile of clenched, gleaming teeth. He was a man who knew how to work a camera, that's for sure.

"In the coming weeks, we will unfold this grandeur of Panligo, but suffice it to say that the bedrock upon which this assembly of the religious affections of the world is founded consists of three unifying principles."

Weiss cleared his throat and sat up straighter. "First, Panligo's aim is to form a nucleus around which the universal brotherhood of humanity can assemble, regardless of race, creed, sex, caste, color, or sexuality—even form, whether human or humanoid. Secondly, we invite the exploration of the various religious, philosophical, and scientific strands within expressions of humanity that seek to explain the ground of our existence and aim of the world community. Finally, Panligo recognizes the remarkable complexity of the universe, in all of its humming potential and welcomes the opportunity to explain the laws of nature and explore the power latent within humanity together, with the revelation-insights of the collective consciousness of the *nooma*, the animating divine spark that sits at the heart of all the religions, all of humanity, the entirety of the universe."

The man of white drew his face to a serious pose, pinching his brow together and pursing his lips, leaning in ever-so-slightly toward the camera.

He continued, "For as we all know, we are estranged from the ground of our being, because we are estranged from the origin and aim of our life. Estranged from the very taproot of our existence from the Spirit of the Universe that is God himself. The name of this infinite and inexhaustible depth from whence every atom of the universe flows and the ground of all things that are held together is God. That which we name as God is what all humans across the ages have signified as that which gives meaning to our existence. It points to ultimate reality. Which, as Bishop Abasi noted, has been felt and noticed and named by countless religious prophets through the ages.

The Spirit, the Breath, the *Nooma* that flows through every conscious being in Solterra—man or machine—imbuing them with ultimate meaning."

"That dude is seriously off his rocker," Ford said, pealing a banana the man had stowed away somewhere in his GI-Joe combat suit.

Weiss closed his eyes and inhaled a long breath, his nostrils flaring and white head tilting back slightly, as if entering into some sort of ecstatic trance. With eyes still closed, he said, "Panligo seeks to embrace religious, philosophical, and scientific truth as it is found in all sources. It is a great unifier and peacemaker in religion, establishing a brotherhood of all faith in which the united peoples of Solterra can also come together to unite around the one Spirit that binds us all together in the unity of the bonds of peace."

He snapped his eyes open again and smiled widely. "It is profoundly religious, as it teaches the essential truths found in all religions. For as we can all agree: *Omnia est unum et unum est omnibus!*"

"Oh, good Lord…" Father Jim complained.

"What's that, Latin?" asked Ford.

Alexander nodded. Folding his arms, he said. "*All is One, and One is All.*"

The man scoffed, popping a piece of his banana in his mouth. "Sounds more like a frat-club motto than a religious creed."

He agreed. And one that his best friend was now openly embracing.

With that, the feed cut to black.

CHAPTER 8

The DiviNet connection cut to the Solterra logo of a spinning globe, the land masses fitted together like a jigsaw puzzle and surrounded by olive branches.

Ford was the first to speak. "What kind of cockamamy bull was that?" he said, biting into his banana again.

"Stuff and nonsense, is what that was!" Father Jim scoffed.

Alexander had to agree. Although some of the contours of what both Abasi and Weiss said echoed inklings of what he himself had wondered the past few months amidst the overwhelming demands of ministering to his people and the culture that pressed so militantly against what Ichthus held dear.

Arms still folded and staring at the blank display, he said, "But what does it mean?"

Father Jim mirrored Alexander, crossing his arms in contemplation with brow furrowed. "Haven't a clue, dear fellow," he mumbled. "But there is a ring to it that strikes me as dark and ominous, as if the Church has rounded this bend a time or two."

"What are you thinking, Padre?" Alexander said. "What was Weiss and..." he trailed off, his stomach lurching and breath growing shallow as he voiced the truth of the matter. "And Abasi—what were they talking about?"

Father Jim looked up, his face looking gaunt. "Not sure, my boy. Not sure. Which calls for a little trip to the Archives, I'd say. Come along."

Without waiting for his companions, he stood and strode forward with purpose, slinging open the reinforced door to the ops center and leaving the others to follow.

Alexander followed after him; Ford was close behind. Father Jim rounded a corner to the right farther up the hallway from where they had originally come. He hustled up to his mentor's side as the man continued down the long corridor to a pair of doors up ahead, his face set with a mixture of determination and contemplation.

"Ah, here we are," Father Jim said, stopping at an ornately patterned door in carved vines and whorls, a similar entry pad and biometric scanner affixed to the right on the wall.

"You said *Archives*," Alexander whispered as the cardinal went through the now-familiar routine. "It's not what I think it is, is it?"

There was a *ping* of success and an audible unlocking of the door. The cardinal grasped the handle and turned. "And what might that be?" He winked and hefted open the door, then held it for his companions.

Alexander hesitated, but followed his direction, as did Ford. Both of their brows furrowed at what they saw, releasing a collective gasp of surprise.

The room was about the size of a gymnasium, its floor paved with large black-and-white tiles and lined down the center with solid squat columns supporting a vaulted ceiling that arched two or three stories high. Lining the columns were frescoes of saints. Splashed across the white ceiling were more frescos of celestial beings and brightly colored patterns of greens and reds and blues. Many of the walls continued the theme, portraying scenes from the Old Testament and the Gospels. A few others displayed spine-out books neatly arrayed on darkly stained wood shelves. Gilded tables sat in between the columns, mounted by glowing green banker's lamps. It smelled of fresh sanitized air, with the hint of an old library filled with must and paper. A fire crackled at one end, giving off spicy smoke that mingled with the old-world scent. The sights and smells brought back instant memories of his time at Oxford studying in the well-preserved Bodleian Library.

But what the heck was a library doing in Nicaea? Especially in a world where books had been virtually banned—the paper kind, anyway?

After the Reckoning, real books were hard to come by. Deforestation for paper production was a strict no-no that carried significant monetary and hard-labor penalties. So digital was the way the biblio-world went. Alexander was one of many who suspected the Republic outlawed paper production for means other than merely environmental protection: Information was much easier to control when it was in ones and zeros rather than ink and parchment. Who needed book burnings when they could be evaporated with a simple command input from the Regis, Lucius Severus, or an AI algorithmic command line?

Ford whistled, craning his neck for a look around. "Nice digs ya got here, chief."

Alexander looked on with the same awe, then scoffed and said, "What, you didn't know about this?"

He shrugged. "I'm the new guy. Still getting acclimated."

"What is this place?"

"Why, the Vatican Archives." Both men snapped their necks toward Father Jim, eyes wide with stunned confusion. "Well, most of it anyway."

"I thought the Archives drowned in the sea. That's what OneWorld News itself reported."

"That's what the Ministerium *wanted* OneWorld News to report. And some of the precious manuscripts and documents and codices of the Church's past did unfortunately succumb to Poseidon's clutches. But Ichthus transferred the most important and vast majority of them here for, shall we say, safekeeping."

Alexander couldn't believe it. Ichthus had preserved her historic memory after all. All of the records from councils and papal bulls, the books on doctrine and practice. He imagined Solterra would have a conniption if they knew they had been saved and stowed away for safekeeping.

What other secrets was Ichthus hiding? What was Father Jim himself hiding?

He furrowed his brow and squinted an eye, then turned to the cardinal. "Wait a minute. I thought you said the chamber beneath the Church of the Dormition was created only recently for the purposes of the conclave. But if the Vatican Archives were saved, and the frescoes from the Sistine Chapel for the conclave chamber itself were saved, then this place would have to have been built decades ago. And that room we just came from seemed like some...nerve center out of one of those cheap electronic thrillers. What's going on here, Padre? Where are we?"

Father Jim looked to Ford, who nodded.

Which irritated Alexander. The man was clearly privy to whatever the heck was going on in a way that he wasn't.

The cardinal nodded and said, "It is true, as you say it. Ichthus spent the better part of a decade constructing this place as a sort of command center, as you put it. And frankly, a retreat for Ichthus when times went dim. We needed a place outside the prying eyes and listening ears of the Republic to conduct Church business and further Christ's mission in the world. Not to mention preserving Ichthus and the faith. It is indeed a much larger complex than I had originally led you to believe a week ago. And this space," he said, sweeping his arms around, "is at the center of it all."

"This?" Alexander asked. "Not the tricked-out room of techno gadgets and displays? And what is this room, anyway? Looks like some sort of study area from the Vatican Library. The Sistine Hall, if I'm not mistaken."

Father Jim raised a brow and grinned. "Impressive, Father Zarruq. But slight correction: a faux Sistine Hall of the Vatican Library."

Alexander craned his neck again, eyeing the space. "Looks real to me."

"It's been programmed to look that way, giving the appearance of the once fabled hall."

"Programmed?" asked Ford.

"Indeed. Go ahead, inspect the walls. Touch them even."

Alexander furrowed his brow in confusion, then took a step up to a column with a tall, bearded man wearing a red toga and bearing a book. He squinted at its surface, noticing a sheen to it and what looked like faint pixilation. He brought his hand up to the surface, hesitated, and then touched it. Smooth as glass. He pressed a finger against it. The image instantly rippled with red, blue, and green perturbation, like a stone dropped in a pond.

"I don't understand," he said. "What's the point of it?"

"The point, my dear fellow, is to offer the Ministerium instant access to a billion-book digital archive from the storehouses of the Church's knowledge. Just watch."

Father Jim took a step forward and cleared his throat. "Qoheleth, bring me a selection of books on J. Gresham Machen."

Alexander smiled at the call word, *Qoheleth*. The purported author of the book of Ecclesiastes.

"Granted," a male Britannia-sounding voice echoed. The room instantly transformed into a selection of spine-out titles neatly arrayed across the walls of the vast space.

Ford whistled again. "Now that there is some fine Ichthus ingenuity."

"Come, come," the cardinal said, walking over to one of the gilded tables. He retrieved a sapphire slate before heading for the shelves of digital titles arrayed on one panel.

Alexander quickly followed him, eager to see what it was the Church had manufactured.

"Now, watch and learn," Father Jim said.

He brought the sapphire tablet near a particular set of tomes that lined the wall on the middle shelf. The others surrounding it seemed to instantly dim, while three remained brightly lit. Father Jim touched the middle volume, and the others joined the other books in dimmed darkness. He tapped it again, and it shone with an almost golden brilliance, a faint halo of rainbow light ringing it.

"There we go," the cardinal announced. He turned his tablet to face the two men. On its surface was the cover of a book titled *Christianity and Liberalism,* by a one J. Gresham Machen. The man he had commanded Qoheleth to summon.

"Sweetness," Ford whispered, stepping closer to the tablet and grabbing it from Father Jim.

Alexander had to agree. It was a sweet trick. "I presume we can pluck any old book to our heart's content?"

Father Jim nodded. "Indeed. The digital archives have preserved knowledge of all sorts during these dark times. Not just that which had been contained in the Vatican Archives before it sank beneath the sea, but all books from every corner of the world. As you'll recall, it was the Church that preserved knowledge through the so-called Dark Ages—a misnomer if there ever was one! The Renaissance was only made possible by the studious and judicious care with which Christians sought, discovered, and preserved the wisdom that God himself ordained his creatures to possess."

"Hence *Qoheleth*," said Alexander, "the bearer of the wisdom found in the book of Ecclesiastes in the Hebrew Scriptures, the Old Testament."

"Exactly," Father Jim said, grinning proudly. "That was my addition."

"Well, what do we do with this here doohickey?" asked Ford, eyeing the tablet. "And why can't we just summon the catalogs from the slate?"

"You can. But it isn't as intuitive of an interface as directly engaging with the Archives shelves."

"And besides, what would be the fun in that?" replied Alexander.

"Precisely. If I may..." Father Jim took back the tablet and began flipping through the book. The cardinal cleared his throat, then read: "'*Light may seem at times to be an impertinent intruder, but it is always beneficial in the end. The type of religion which rejoices in the pious sound of traditional phrases, regardless of their meanings, or shrinks from 'controversial' matters, will never stand amid the shocks of life.*'"

"Ain't that the truth," Ford said, stuffing the rest of his banana in his mouth and the expended peal in a pocket.

"'*In the sphere of religion, as in other spheres,*'" the cardinal continued, "'*the things about which men are agreed are apt to be the things that are least worth holding; the really important things are the things about which men will fight.*'"

Father Jim smiled with satisfaction and handed the tablet to Alexander. "J. Gresham Machen," he said with admiration. "Now there was a fighter of the faith, if there ever was one. The old professor of New Testament studies from Princeton Seminary who led a conservative revolt against those who wished to change the meaning of what it meant to be Christian, as they still called the faith back in those days at the start of the twentieth century. Very instructive."

He turned to Alexander and to Ford. "Which brings us to this room. It gives us access to nearly the entire storehouse of knowledge across the full spectrum of humanity. Using machine learning algorithms, the Archives not only catalogues but cross-checks the vault of knowledge with other bits and bobs of information and sources. And Solterra thinks we're just a bunch of rubes stuck in the Stone Age." Father Jim huffed and shook his head. "At any rate, it's quite simple, really. You walk over to the shelves and search for your book. As you saw, when you find it, simply tap once, then again for it to be instantly delivered to the device. It's quite magical, really. And here we have a bit more about what we may be up against."

"Which is what, exactly?" asked Alexander.

"That's where Qoheleth comes into play."

Father Jim cleared his throat, then said, "Qoheleth, would you cross-check the recent live-stream video of Josiah Abasi from DiviNet with the Archives, searching for anything that might connect that will give us some bloody clue as to what Panligo might be up to?"

"Granted," the male voice said again.

"Wow, it can do that, chief?" Ford said. "Just like that—speak to it and it does your bidding?"

"Exactly."

"I need to get me one of those."

A *purr* sounded, indicating Qoheleth had worked its magic. The walls shifted again, transforming the shelves of books back into the original frescos except for a single section with an arrangement of books.

"Let's have ourselves a look at what our friend discovered."

The trio approached the wall, eyeing the spines with names and titles Alexander hadn't heard of before.

Father Jim smacked his hand against his forehead. "That's right! I knew I recognized those dog whistles from somewhere."

"Care to fill us in?" Alexander asked.

"It's called Theosophy."

"Theo-what?" Ford wondered, brow furrowed with confusion.

"Theosophy."

"Wisdom of God?" Alexander said, recalling his Greek training.

Father Jim nodded. "Literally, *divine wisdom*. It was a pseudo-spiritual movement that formed in the late-nineteenth century and found purchase throughout the twentieth and twenty-first centuries in the West. It was equal parts religious, philosophical, and scientific. And really, a pantheistic form of ancient Gnosticism, is what it was."

"Never heard of it."

"It was arguably the most influential occult doctrine of the late nineteenth century, after its first society dedicated to the neo-spiritualism was founded in New York City in 1875. The alternative spiritual sect drew heavily from the religions of the East, Hinduism and Buddhism. It was also rooted in Darwinism and Egyptian religion. But the real innovation was its genuine attempt to combine natural science and supernaturalism, rationalism and mysticism into a coherent set of teachings. And, as you heard voiced just now, the alternative spirituality advocated for the progressive, cosmopolitan belief in forming a universal brotherhood of all races, creeds, castes, and colors. Ironically, though, it was also aimed at bringing a so-called sixth root race into existence that was thoroughly Indo-European."

"A root race?" Alexander questioned. "Sounds fascist."

"Indeed, it was. The movement quickly found purchase throughout the old German and Austrian nation-states, which incorporated more overtly racialist and imperialist elements into the fold. A few prominent fellows within Germany founded the German chapter, even finding favor with members of the Third Reich."

"The Third Reich?" Ford exclaimed. "As in, like, Nazi Germany?"

Alexander raised a brow and laughed. "Know of any other Third Reich members, genius?"

Cheap shot, but he sort of liked taking it. It was silly, but he didn't care for the guy. Too macho and walked with too much of a swagger for his liking. Made him feel small and weak. Like back in secondary school when the jocks mocked him mercilessly for being overweight. He'd showed them all up now. Trim and lean, but still uncoordinated with anything requiring agility and strength, like sports. Or the Solterra military.

He sighed and cursed himself for being a jerk, thirsting for a ribbon of relief from the pack of narcowafers nestled at the bottom of his pocket.

Father Jim cleared his throat and threw Alexander a look. "Several prominent theosophists had come to the movement through occult circles seeking a path that unified scientific materialism and religious supernaturalism. It purported to embrace the reality that a truth stood above the world religions and sought answers to unexplained natural laws and powers within humanity. Spiritualism, clairvoyance, telepathy, and parapsychology were mainstays of the movement."

"Boy, doesn't that pile of straw sound familiar," Ford said, folding his arms and widening his stance.

"Obviously, we heard some of that from Abasi, of all people. Lord save his soul," the cardinal mumbled and crossed himself. "These earlier practitioners dedicated themselves to bridging the gap between natural science with a spiritual awakening that would befit the modern, industrial age, synthesizing knowledge and belief into an End Times vision of humanity's history and future. Which was then entirely co-opted by the Nazis in their völkisch, Ario-Germanic ideology."

"Wicked."

"Indeed."

"And apparently resurrected," Alexander added.

The other two nodded in grim agreement.

Silence settled over the room as they contemplated the gravity of what they had witnessed, what had begun to be unleashed upon the world. Upon Ichthus.

Ford broke that silence: "I'd say it's time to kick Project 65 into high gear. Pay our little hermit a visit."

"Perhaps it is..." Father Jim agreed.

Alexander glanced at Ford before turning to his mentor. "What's he talking about? What hermit? And what's Project 65?"

Father Jim took in a deep breath and pulled out a chair from one of the gilded tables, motioning for the two to do the same. He leaned back, saying nothing as they took their seats.

"Do you want to do the honors? Or shall I?" Ford said, sticking his hands in his pockets and slouching back in his chair.

Several seconds ticked by before the cardinal leaned forward and answered. "Do you recall the conclave after-party from a week ago, Alex?"

"After-party?" Alexander said, shaking his head and furrowing his brow.

"The discussion about options to solve the emerging crisis surrounding Panligo and Weiss and Nicolai."

"You mean about Sasha and time travel?"

"Before that."

Alexander shook his head in confusion, then it dawned on him. He looked from Padre to Ford, then back again. "Are you talking about the lost religious order that Mother Amara mentioned? The Order of Thaddeus?"

The door to the Archives at the other end thudded open, intercepting Father Jim's response. One of the personnel in a light gray uniform matching John Mark Ford's strode across the room, his rubber military boots squeaking on the marble flooring.

The ex-military man from Solterra jumped up and strode forward to meet the man, the two meeting in the middle and the one personnel promptly saluting him.

Ford said, "At ease, soldier. What's wrong?"

"We've got a situation," the man echoed across the room.

"Of course we do," Father Jim mumbled.

CHAPTER 9

"Well, speak up, lad," Father Jim complained as he joined the two men. "I shan't think this bag of bones is getting any younger under your tied tongue."

The man's head fell slightly, his face reddening. Then he cleared his throat and said, "There's been an infiltration."

"A what?"

Ford held up a hand, taking the situation back in his control. "Ruben, what do you mean by *infiltration?*"

The man snapped back to attention. "Someone entered the perimeter of the church and…" He trailed off, hanging his head again and rubbing the back of his neck.

"Spit it out, soldier."

Ruben swallowed. "They managed to breach the sub-layer beneath the structure that leads to the Ministerium, and they were found lurking outside a sensitive part of the compound."

"How the bloody hell did they manage that?" Father Jim exclaimed. "We've taken great pains to keep this place from the watching world—not to mention secreting it away from the prying eyes of the Republic! No one was supposed to know. Not the Republic, and certainly not some *lurker*, as you put it. Whoever the bloody hell they are."

Alexander furrowed his brow at the cardinal. That was news to him. Far as he knew, it was just a meeting location for Ministerium business. When he had been brought to the conclave a week ago, it had seemed the secret was the meeting itself. Not the whereabouts of the meeting.

But with the command center and the ex-military Ford, combined with the military-looking personnel he saw earlier and now this guy—it looked like the secret was the fact the governing body of Ichthus was secreted away, and guarded by mercenaries no less!

"Have you begun the interrogation?" asked Ford.

"We've...exchanged words, yes."

"And who is he? Where did he come from?"

"He is a *she*."

"She?"

The man shrugged. "Claims to be part of the Ministerium security, but it's clearly a ruse."

Ford glanced at Alexander before looking to Father Jim.

"Well, don't wait for my go-ahead," the cardinal said. "Get on with it!"

He nodded, then turned to Ruben. "Take me to her."

The trio followed the man out the door and back down the hall they had been through earlier. Only now it was dead, cleared of all personnel. Alexander imagined it had something to do with the security protocol after the incident.

They rounded a bend and walked straight toward a set of double doors. Ford moved past the man leading the group and slapped his hand against the security pad and shoved his face in front of the scanner. Within a few seconds, the door unlocked and he shoved through.

Father Jim hesitated before following. He said to Alexander, "Understand that Ichthus has taken measures during these extreme world circumstances the past decade since the Reckoning to ensure the survival of the Church. Do you understand what I'm saying?"

Alexander took an uncertain breath. No, not entirely. But he had a feeling he was being brought into the inner world of the Ministerium that only the one percent had any clue existed. He wasn't sure he wanted the invitation.

Instead, he nodded. "I understand. Complete non-disclosure. Got it."

"Right. In we go."

Father Jim led the two through the doors and into a more brightly lit hallway that was cooler and more sanitized than the other one. Up ahead, there were voices arguing, Ford's and the other man's.

And a woman.

Who sounded vaguely familiar...

They followed the shouting to another hallway and then toward a room that was shining more brightly than the hallway itself. A holding room. Just four walls, cinder blocks painted white, with bright white LED light. Sitting on a metal chair at the center was a woman he recognized with olive skin and close-cropped black hair wearing black clothes, arms and wrists bound to the chair with steel clasps. Father Jim recognized her too.

"Tara Rodriguez?" he said with gasping surprise.

The other two men turned their heads toward the cardinal.

"Finally!" Tara exclaimed.

"What is the meaning of this?" asked Father Jim.

"You know her?" Ford wondered.

"Of course! Don't you?"

His eyes widened, his face reddened. He heaved in a breath and blew it out. "In a word: no."

Father Jim huffed an exasperated breath. "She's part of the very operational apparatus you're head over, for goodness' sake! Although, admittedly a wing that's responsible for the Fidelium."

Ford put his hands on his hips. "Well, I'll be."

"Don't just stand there," the cardinal said to the man in gray. "Release her, would you?"

Ruben shuffled forward, fumbling with a set of keys.

"I'd say that's a fine kettle of fish you've gotten us into there, Ruben," Ford said.

"Speak for yourself," Alexander said under his breath, angered at such a screwup with the woman who had taken care of him a week ago, bringing him safely to the conclave.

"Ms. Rodriguez, what the blazes happened here?" Father Jim asked with exasperation.

"Sorry, sir," Ruben said as he worked to release the clasps securing her arms. "This is all my fault. I assumed she was an intruder after finding her lurking around the entrance to the servers—"

"I was doing no such thing!" she interrupted, pointing at the man in gray with her one released arm. When she did, something peeked out underneath her black sleeve.

Alexander sucked in a breath of recognition at the sight.

Wait a minute...

A faint pair of intersecting black lines, the ends bent at odd angles, rested on the underside of her wrist.

Tara threw him a glance, then pulled down her sleeve.

A memory raced to the surface of his consciousness, causing him to hold his breath at its surprising revelation—as if exhaling would give himself away for what he knew.

The tattoo!

Those lines looked mysteriously like the pair he had

glimpsed on the arm of the person he had tumbled into coming down the path outside his parish before it—

Alexander took a step back from the group, then another, folding his arms at his chest and hanging his head with confused contemplation.

But it can't be...

A thousand questions and thoughts jumbled together as he remembered that moment: coming up the hill to return home after the harrowing adventure going to the conclave; the stampede into the chamber by Weiss and Nicolai and others; traveling through time to retrieve the words from the Apostle John.

All before he smacked into the figure barreling down the pathway to his parish like a bat out of hell that bore that bird tattoo!

Father Jim chuckled. "Obviously, there was a bit of a misunderstanding here, Tara."

She scoffed. "I'd say."

"A thousand apologies," Ruben offered.

"I told you who I was, numbskull," Tara said as the man in gray finished releasing her bonds.

"Well, how the heck was I supposed to know you were telling the truth?"

"How the heck did you think I got into the Ministerium in the first place, Sherlock? And who the heck did you think I was, anyhow?"

The man shrugged then quickly, and wisely, backed away as she went to stand.

"Terribly sorry, ma'am," Ford said, offering her his hand.

She glanced at it as she rubbed her wrists where they had been secured to the chair, then smiled. "I think I'll pass."

He took in a breath and reddened, then joined Ruben's side.

Tara stood and glanced back at the pair before walking to the door. "And you're the new head of operations I've heard about? Sheesh..." She shook her head and mumbled something, then left.

"My dear fellows," Father Jim said, taking her seat. "Now there's a sticky wicket, if I've ever seen one."

Ford clenched his jaw and gave Ruben a biting look. "Out. I'll deal with you later."

Ruben opened his mouth, as if mustering up a defense. But he said nothing, instead following Tara's lead out the door.

Alexander glanced at the door and considered what he had seen on the arm of the woman who had just walked through it. Two intersecting lines, bent at odd angles, resembling a bird.

Like the figure who had dashed down the path just moments before his church exploded in a phantasmic show of hellish fire and fury.

His chest tightened and breathing became more difficult; his heart was hammering in his head at the revelation he could barely come to grips with, stoking a question he dared not ask.

Was Tara responsible for the persecuting terror that befell his beloved parish?

"Something the matter, Alex?" asked Father Jim.

"Huh?" he said, whipping his head toward the cardinal.

"You look like you've been visited by a poltergeist, the way your face is creased and eyes all ablaze with fright."

Alexander said nothing, his mind still fixated on that cruel question.

A hum from the lights above filled the void.

Ford took a step forward; Father Jim glanced at him. The two shared a confused look.

"Father Zarruq..." Father Jim said.

"Huh?" Alexander said again.

The cardinal stood and chuckled. "One more round of this

and I'm going to tell John Mark, here, to strap you to the chair and do to you what that lad Ruben was about to do to Tara! Now what on earth is the matter?"

Alexander glanced at Ford. The man's eyes were narrowed into a look of probing inquiry. He said nothing, but his face told Alexander he was about to be forced to talk if he didn't get to it.

Bowing his head, he said, "So, there's something I neglected to tell you, Padre."

"Something you neglected to tell me?" Father Jim said. "I don't understand. What are you saying?"

He hesitated, his mind swimming from the confusion of it all.

"Go on," Ford said gently, his eyes still bearing that transfixed look of interrogation.

Alexander shifted, his mouth watering for a narcowafer and fingers tingling to reach for one. Finally, he said, "The evening that my parish was terrorized—that it was...bombed." He stopped to swallow and take a breath. "Right before it exploded, I was coming up the path that led to my parish and I ran into someone."

"Ran into someone?" Father Jim said. "In what way?"

"In the way that it sounds. I was walking home, not looking where I was going, and someone came running down the other way and we collided."

"Who?" asked Ford, taking a step closer.

Alexander shook his head. "I'm not sure. But the thing about it is, I caught sight of something on their wrist."

He paused, the hum of lights offering the only reply to his silence.

He continued, "It was some sort of tattoo. Two intersecting lines, the ends bent at odd angles."

Ford sighed and shifted, folding his arms and tightening his gaze on Alex.

"I'm sorry, my boy," Father Jim said, "but what does any of this have to do with Ms. Rodriguez?"

Alexander opened his mouth to answer but couldn't voice a reply.

"You saw it, didn't you?" Ford answered for him. "The tattoo on Tara."

He took a breath, nodding his reply instead.

"What?" Father Jim said, standing with exclamation.

Alexander folded his arms and said nothing.

Ford rubbed his chin and whistled but said nothing more.

Father Jim looked at Ford, mouth agape. Then he turned back to Alexander. "Do you really think Tara had something to do with the attack on your church?"

He paused a beat and took a breath. "All I know is, minutes before my parish exploded, I ran into someone barreling down the path who had some sort of markings that looked eerily similar to what Tara looked like she had on her wrist."

"But that makes no sense! Ms. Rodriquez has been helping shield us from the Republic's gaze. Came personally recommended from an old family friend."

Ford took out a notebook and pen from a zipped pocket. He opened it to a blank page and twisted the cap off the pen, then handed them to Alexander. "Here. Draw what you saw. Both what you saw at your parish before the bombing and...well, what you think you saw on Tara's wrist."

Alexander hesitated, but took them and started drawing what he had witnessed in both instances. Sure, beyond a doubt, that they matched.

He handed the notebook and pen back to Ford. The man eyed the drawing, then frowned. "Check this out, chief?"

Furrowing his brow, Father Jim took the notebook. Then he gasped with recognition.

"Dear me," he said, slumping down in Tara's chair again.

"You recognize this drawing?"

"I'm afraid I do. And it is entirely germane to our previous discussion."

"Which one?" asked Alexander.

"The one about Project 65."

CHAPTER 10

Ford led the way out of the holding area, followed by Father Jim and Alexander. Winding back through the sanitized hallways of slate gray and dim recessed lighting now filled with the normal rhythm and rumble of personnel, soon they came to a set of doors with the familiar security apparatus.

This time, Father Jim did the honors. He moved to the entrance and applied his palm to a scanner resting to the right. A beat later, the door unlocked with a click and the cardinal pushed through—taking them into a room oddly familiar.

It was similar in size and shape as the Archives, the floor paved with the same large square black-and-white tiles. The squat pillars were missing, but similar frescos with scenes from the Bible lined the walls in addition to scenes of martyrdom and evangelism from the early Church. Splashed across the white ceiling were more frescos of the same celestial beings and brightly colored patterns they had witnessed before. Another fire crackled at one end, giving off the same spicy smoke that mingled with the same old world musty scent of paper, this time with the added scent of old plaster. Before it stood a grouping of gilded cloth couches with fine embroidery.

Commanding the center of the room was a large oak table piled high with ancient-looking tomes and manuscripts.

"Where are we?" Alexander wondered as they walked toward the table.

"The real Sistine Hall of the Vatican Library. Or, at least what's left of it. When the architects of the chamber we visited a week ago for the conclave removed the remnants of the Sistine Chapel to reconstruct it underground before the seas gulped down the Vatican beneath its waters, they also took great pains to remove the frescos and ornamentation and other architectural accouterments of various Vatican buildings. Not only did they preserve the important sacred texts of Ichthus from the library, they also preserved the frescos and furniture. Some of what you saw on the walls of the Archives were those in digital form. These are the real ones, expertly brought to this study."

"Your study, I presume?"

Father Jim grinned and winked as they reached the center table. "A man needs comfortable accommodations if he's to solve the Church's problems."

"I guess so."

Alexander took in the display before him on the table, his head filling with the dizzying scent of old paper. He eyed a piece of parchment resting on a cleared space in the table surrounded by stacks of books. A magnifying glass was resting on it, as if it had been handled recently. He carefully bent forward with his hands behind his back for a closer look.

"Go ahead, take it," said Father Jim.

"Are you sure? It looks like it could disintegrate in my hands."

"Oh, I think it's safe to say there's nothing to worry about after the journey it's been on through the millennia."

"Millennia?" Alexander startled, glancing at him with a look of confusion.

"Mm-hmm. Go on. Take a look."

He hesitated, but removed the magnifying glass and moved in to take the parchment. He wiggled his fingers under the ancient manuscript, then inched his palms farther underneath it to carefully pick it up. He leaned in, then slowly brought it closer to his face for inspection.

Scrawled in neat lines across the parchment were what looked to be Koine Greek, the ancient tongue of the first followers of Jesus during the first century. It was faint, the once-dark black having faded over the centuries, but he could make out some of the letters and then words:

IOUDASINSOUXRISTOUDOULOS

The Greeks had originally written words together in strings of capital letters without punctuation or breaks. This parchment must have been truly ancient to have preserved such a form. Recalling some of his training during graduate school for the priesthood, he began translating in his head, following the letters and putting in mental breaks on his own:

Jude, a slave of Jesus Christ...

Alexander sucked in a startled breath. His eyes went wide, and he turned to Father Jim. "Is this the Epistle of Jude?"

"I see you've still got your translating chops. And yes, indeed it is."

"How cool is that..." The parchment seemed to grow in weight at the understanding that he was holding a near-original copy of a book from the Holy Scriptures.

"This has to be, what, from the fourth century? Codex Sinaiticus, perhaps?"

Father Jim grinned. "Oh dear, far older than that."

"Third century?" Alexander asked still eyeing the beautiful piece of Church history resting in his hands.

"Nope. Older still."

He turned to the cardinal and raised a brow. "Second?"

The man chuckled and crossed his arms. "What would you say if I were to tell you this is an original of Jude's letter—*the* original letter he wrote to churches in Asia Minor struggling under the weight of violating teaching and persecuting violence?"

Alexander coughed and nearly fumbled the ancient manuscript at the revelation. He promptly eased it back to the table for safekeeping.

"Original? As in, the very letter Jude Thaddeus wrote way back when?"

Father Jim grinned. "That would be the one."

His jaw literally dropped, and he let out a dumbfounded breath. "But how?"

"It was preserved across the centuries by a little-known religious order that has served crucial purposes throughout the life of Ichthus."

"Really? Which one?"

"*Ordo Thaddeum*," Father Jim said.

Alexander tilted his head and furrowed his brow. "Order of Thaddeus?"

"Indeed."

"Isn't that the religious order Mama Mara mentioned."

Father Jim nodded, saying nothing.

Alexander didn't know anything about this lost order. Then it hit him.

"Ah, Project 65. The sixty-fifth letter of the Church's Scriptures. The Epistle of Jude. Tradition has it that the disciple who wrote the letter to the churches of Asia Minor was known as Jude Thaddeus, the apostle of Christ mentioned in the Gospels, isn't that right?"

"Right you are. And it's not surprising you haven't heard of the order."

"*Lost* order, you mean?"

Father Jim hesitated, looking to Ford. The man folded his arms and widened his stance, then nodded. "Yes, well, we'll get to that. But through the centuries, and especially two-hundred years ago, the Order had been working in the shadows, protecting and preserving the memory of the Church from nearly the very beginning of her existence."

Alexander considered this. "And the name Thaddeus...I'm guessing there's some sort of link between him and the order's founding?"

"Exactly. He was, in fact, the founder of the order. Like the Franciscans, named after Saint Francis of Assisi, and the Benedictines who are named after Saint Benedict of Nursia."

Alexander scoffed. "Seriously? From what I understand, orders of the Church, well the ones we know of, weren't around in the first century. The first one didn't even officially launch until the early Middle Ages. The Order of Saint Benedict, one of the earliest and most enduring, wasn't it?"

"Officially, you are right," Father Jim acknowledged. "Unofficially, Thaddeus, or Saint Jude as he is also known, the patron saint of lost causes, was acutely aware of the forces already pressing in against the Church and the teachings of the faith. Just look at his letter! Jude told the Christians living in a highly oppressed region of the Roman Empire that he wanted to write to them about their wonderful salvation in Jesus. However, a more urgent matter caught his attention."

Alexander frowned and returned to the parchment. Leaning over it, he searched its sentences, his eyes alighting on a string of Koine Greek characters:

---

*EPAGONIZESTHAITN'APAXPARADOTHEIS-
NTOIS' AGIOISPISTE*

The ends of his mouth tugged upward; his eyes welled with the revelation embedded in those words—those *original* words, apparently.

"'*Contend for the faith that was once for all entrusted to God's holy people,*'" Alexander mumbled.

He had memorized the verse early in his Christian journey. He was drawn to its passion, to its conviction that there was an essence to the Christian faith that needed to be contended for, preserved—protected even. It was one of those life verses that propelled him through his training to be a priest and gave rise to his ministry in the face of a culture that had disintegrated to a mirror image of first-century Rome and a Church that had lost its way fighting against the rising tide overwhelming her.

Alexander sighed and shook his head. Those were the days. When a fire burned in his belly to join the ranks of those who had contended for the once-for-all Ichthus faith. When he sought to buttress the seawall around the City on a Hill that served as a beacon of hope in the midst of the darkening—make that *darkened*—world.

Now...Now he had lost his parish—the people of his parish, not to mention the building of his parish. But it was more than that: The passion that had once fueled his faith and ministry had been hard to come by lately. Like grasping for oil in water, that passion had been slipping through his fingers. And now he felt spent, passion*less*. Like too little of the jam he made from the berries that grew along the bluff of his parish spread across too much bread.

"You're exactly right, my boy," Father Jim said, bringing

him back to the moment. "Contend. Fight for. Preserve and protect. Not only the faith itself, but the shared, collective *memory* of the faith."

He nodded toward the grouping of couches near the fire and started shuffling toward them.

He continued, "Jude Thaddeus had already seen evidence for the need to preserve and protect this memory. And, remember, this was within decades of the phenomenon of the Church launching from that Pentecost day. Within years of the Jesus movement launching and elements of the faith already being taught and memorized and recited—within years it was beginning to fray at the edges, nearly busting at the seams from the threat of false teaching from within, not to mention from the persecuting violence of Empire Rome and the Jewish authorities coming at her from the outside. That was bad enough, what with the beheadings and crucifixions and death-by-lion-maulings in the Colosseum."

Father Jim took a breath as they reached their destination, sinking hard into one of the gilded chairs tastefully embroidered with lines of blue and red and green. Alexander took a similar chair across from him; Ford took the couch between them across from the crackling fire.

The cardinal continued, "But the more devious and dastardly and dangerous threat was on the inside from false teachers penetrating the fragile, nascent People of the Way, as they were known. Those who had pledged their allegiance to Lord Christ, believing in faith that Jesus had paid the price for their sins in their place, had risen from the dead to new life, and ascended in glory to the right hand of the Father—all the while entrusting their lives to his care and eternal protection. In his letter, Jude Thaddeus warned against the people who wanted to pervert the message of God's grace into a license for immorality and to deny Jesus Christ our only Savior and Lord."

This was getting heavy. And confusing. What did any of this have to do with the Ministerium?

"So let me see if I got this straight," Alexander said. "Jude Thaddeus, apostle of Jesus Christ and author of what we know as the Epistle of Jude, formed a religious order to contend for the Church and Christian faith early on, is that right—what, late first-century?"

"That's right."

"Alright, but what does any of that have to do with AD 2123? And why haven't I ever heard about this so-called religious order until now? And what the heck is Project 65?"

Father Jim glanced at Ford, who nodded his approval.

The cardinal said, "Project 65 is a clandestine mission within the Ministerium to locate the Order of Thaddeus, reactivate it, and leverage it once again to contend for, preserve, protect, and, most importantly, *fight* for Ichthus."

Contend for. Preserve. Protect. And *fight*? This was way beyond what Alexander had signed up for. He wondered what he was even contending for anymore to begin with. Questioned whether the past should be preserved to begin with. Seemed far too regressive for the ultramodern world. And he certainly wasn't a *fighter*.

"And I must say," Ford continued before he could protest, "if what you say is true, that the doodle you drew turned up on someone's wrist flying like a bat out of hell from your parish before it blew to kingdom come—and it was also on the underside of Tara's wrist...Well, then locating and resurrecting the ancient Order is even more of a priority."

"Why is that?" asked Alexander.

"Because it's the calling card for wicked, wicked people."

He scrunched his face in confusion and sat back, looking to Father Jim for understanding.

The man nodded. "John Mark is right. Those intersecting

lines, the imprint of a phoenix, represent an enemy that the Order has been battling from the very inception of Ichthus. An ancient adversary of the Church called Nous."

"Nous?" Alexander said, shaking his head in confusion. "Isn't that Greek for *mind* or *reason?*"

"Divine reason, actually. It's origin is Neoplatonism, stretching back to the early days of the Church. It has gone by many names over the ages. The *mind's eye*, the *inner consciousness* or *inner knowledge.* It is considered to be the original divine principle, the eye of reason for comprehending the divine, leading to higher knowledge and salvation."

"Sounds like the kind of hippy New Agey, utopian mumbo-jumbo peddled by the four corners of Solterra."

Father Jim chuckled. "This isn't Solterra variety. Rather than the twenty-second century, it instead stretches back to the second century, the essence of its worldview being ancient Gnosticism. The very ideology that nearly unhinged Ichthus way back when and has been resurrected in varying iterations since. One of the largest of which was with twentieth-century theosophy and then with a resurgent menace that nearly destroyed the Church over a century ago in a series of assaults against the faith."

Alexander's breathing started picking up pace, his head hammering a mean beat from the mounting pressure of it all. This was getting even heavier than simply a lost religious order. Ancient enemies battling the Church, nearly destroying Ichthus?

He reached for his pocket to check on his stash of narcowafers. His eyes widened slightly with satisfaction.

Thank God he still had his lifeline.

Father Jim continued, "This esoteric self-salvation through inner, divine knowledge has been something of a nemesis to the Church, stretching back to the earliest days of her existence. The earliest heresies were Gnostic in origin, teaching that salvation was reserved for a certain select few who could leverage the spark of spiritual enlightenment hidden within the inner recesses of the universe and who could progress and push the human race forward through self-actualization. Totally at odds with the Church's teachings on God's open invitation for all of rebellious humanity to find rescue from sins and death through childlike faith in Christ alone."

He paused adjusting his posture and mumbling a complaint. "Nous and its various manifestations have all subscribed to *gnostikos*, the central kernel of gnostic teaching, beginning with the basic assumption of the divinity of the individual. The God-within, a God-consciousness that every person bears to greater or lesser degrees. Each person is a God-in-hiding, as they espouse, a physical shell housing the spark of divinity. There is no sovereign God, but lesser spirit-deities and the divineness of humanity itself."

"Friedrich Nietzsche's *übermensch*, from over a century ago," Alexander said, joining in the lecture. "Superman."

"Not superman," Ford corrected. "*Over*man."

Father Jim smiled at his correction. Alexander did not. Though he was impressed the meathead knew of Nietzsche's *übermensch*. Didn't expect that from a former Solterra grunt.

"Well, you're both right. The übermensch of the Germanian philosopher is the essential aim of Nous. In fact, some of the highest-ranking Nazi officers were members. Joseph Goebbels, even Hitler himself. Heinrich Himmler was a Grand Master. Which makes sense because Gnosticism and occultism are closely aligned—and theosophy was an intimate partner with Nazi ideology. Pursuit of spiritual power through ritual magic is a constant theme throughout the history of Nous, in addition to humanistic utopia."

"Fascinating," Alexander whispered, soaking up the deep-knowledge dive.

"Pantheistic to the core, Nousati believe God or the Divine invades all things, living and non-living. And they assume that prehistoric humans enjoyed uninhibited access to the kind of spiritual truth that would bring about a humanistic salvation."

"Sounds a bit like the newly formed Panligo World Assembly," Alexander added.

Father Jim frowned and nodded. "That it does. And Nous is the organizational manifestation of this ancient worldview. An organization that has lain hidden within the shadows of history, waging war against the Church. Oh, it has popped its head up here or there, to be sure. Beginning with Nicolaism in the Book of Revelation, then with Valentinus and Mani and Arius in the early centuries of the early Church. Joseph Smith reflected the Nousati in the early days of original Americana with Mormonism, as did Carl Jung in Europa. And, as I said, a century ago it emerged from the shadows and unleashed a series of attacks against the Church that nearly brought it to its knees."

Silence settled over the room at the revelation, the snaps and pops of the fire the only sound to be heard.

"Nous..." Alexander mumbled, staring at the fire. He looked at Father Jim and said, "That's the organization you're saying extinguished my parish—my people?"

He shrugged. "Not sure. Though it seems that way. Which, if it proves to be true, portends wicked, wicked things, as John Mark said. There is a militancy about Nous that has always threatened the Church and the faith. In the past, Nous struck at the heart of Christian ideas, attempting to undermine the essence of Ichthus by destroying her teachings. Its power and influence has waxed and waned over the centuries and manifested in various ways. The Nousati have taken many forms.

Jude Thaddeus knew this. He knew that even early on the Church needed to take proactive steps to preserve and protect, contend and fight for the memory of the faith."

Father Jim paused, then leaned forward and said, "And I'm sending you both to go fetch it."

CHAPTER 11

"Hold up," Alexander said, standing and raising a hand of protest. "What do you mean, you're sending us to go fetch it?"

Father Jim stood, so did Ford. The cardinal nodded toward him, and said, "As John Mark alluded, we have been working toward locating the lost Order so as to resurrect it for such a time as this. The Church is facing threats from within and without that the Order of Thaddeus navigated for two millennia. And buried in their communal memory must be resources Ichthus can leverage to ameliorate our own changing, challenging circumstances. Especially with the revelation that Nous may have been resurrected for another fight." He took a shaky breath, then added, "The lost Order is our only hope, Alexander, don't you see?"

Alexander closed his eyes and put a hand to his forehead, the anxiety again opening up a fissure of pain and apprehension just behind his eyes. He rubbed it, his mind reeling from yet another ask to enter the fray again for the Church. He wasn't cut out for this.

With measured words, he said, "I understand that, but this is way beyond what I signed up for, Padre. I thought time traveling was about the tallest order you could have asked of me.

Now you're asking me to jump headlong into an ancient war with an enemy I'm not at all equipped to fight? That's a job for Ford and his Solterra Legion military dropouts, not for me. No offense," he offered, turning to Ford.

He shook his head and put up a hand. "None taken. And I have to agree with the guy, Cardinal Ferraro. This sounds like a job for experienced special-ops personnel, not an inexperienced civilian who you couldn't shake a stick at. No offense."

Shake a stick at? I got plenty of value, you Noramericanan hick!

Alexander opened his mouth to reply when Father Jim intercepted. "But it's precisely your newly acquired time travel experience that we need right now, Alex!"

He was caught off guard by Padre's reference to his recent excursion. "What do you mean? Why would my time travel have anything to do with fetching the Order of Thaddeus?"

Ford answered, "Because the 411 on the lost Order has been so dry the trees are beggin' the dogs for some love."

Both men looked at the man with the same furrowed face of confusion.

Father Jim replied, "Yes, well, I think what our Southern gentleman means is that we've had something of it trying to locate the remnant. They seem to have gone underground. Way underground."

"You're talking about the hermit you mentioned earlier?" asked Alexander.

"Exactly. And I have to imagine that having a sit-down with our new favorite apostle, Jude Thaddeus, could yield some important intel for locating what remains of the Order."

Alexander sucked in a breath and raked a hand through his hair. "So you're saying you want me to pay my good buddy Sasha Pavlovich another visit, right? So that I can borrow his contraption again and go back in time to retrieve the memory of

Jude Thaddeus? To retrieve the memory of the Order's founding, or something?"

Father Jim said nothing.

Ford answered, "There had to have been early instructions of where the Order should operate and how it should conduct itself that may lend clues as to where it may have disappeared. Anything at all to give us some sort of lead to go on would be golden."

"And having yourself a chit-chat with the fellow should also do wonders for the rising apostasy plaguing Ichthus of late," Father Jim added. "Getting him to share the occasion of his letter to the struggling churches in former Byzantium will be a real boon for the Church, combined with the testimony to contend for the once-for-all faith given and gifted to Ichthus. So consider your trip a twofer: gaining crucial intel for locating the lost Order and gaining crucial insight into contending for the faith in the face of rising apostasy."

Alexander clenched his stomach with one arm; he thought he was going to retch right then and there thinking about repeating the journey from a few days ago. The other hand reached into his pocket and grasped his locket of narcowafers. His mouth started watering a pavlovian response for the relief inside.

He took a breath and sighed with resignation. The ember that had launched his ministry in the first place, contending for the faith, offered enough of a spark to spur him onward. Maybe entering into the fray of it all was exactly what he needed—to jumpstart his faith that had begun to wither.

"Fine. I'm in."

"Welcome aboard," Ford said, offering Alexander a grin and his hand.

He took it and nodded.

"Splendid!" said Father Jim. "Leave at once for Ukrainski.

No need to tarry, given the emerging circumstances befalling the Church. I just hope Sasha hasn't run off with the golden goose. After your first run of it, he was none too interested in leaving his professional pursuits and taking advantage of our protection."

"That doesn't surprise me," Alexander said. "If I know Sasha, he'll be holed up at his university office in Kiev poring over the data from his contraption and tweaking it to death. I imagine he'll be more than eager to accommodate a second trial run—with me as a guinea pig."

"One more thing," Ford said before the two broke away. "What do we do about Tara?"

"What do you mean?" Father Jim said.

"If what Alexander says is true, that she's sporting a tattoo with a spitin' image of one that Nous has used as a calling card...Let's just say I can't imagine it's a good idea letting her run around here if she's some sort of turncoat operative."

"No, I shan't believe it is. I hear your point, but I also don't want to jump to any conclusions. Sure, we may suspect she has some sort of connection with the ancient enemy of Ichthus. But suspicion is all we have. And I'm not inclined to indict on that flimsy folder of evidence."

"But the bird tattoo," Alexander protested, sure of what he saw. "Besides, she gave me the creeps last week. Something off about her that doesn't seem right."

Father Jim chuckled. "She has that effect on people from time to time. But unless you give me actual proof of her involvement with Nous, with polygraphic evidence and video surveillance and the bloody mystery tattoo staring me in the face, I'm sorry but we need to sit tight, watching and waiting for more."

The two men sighed with resignation but nodded in agreement.

"Roger, roger, chief," Ford said. "We'll rendezvous with this Doc Pavlovich character and see if we can't get ourselves a good ol' fashioned time travel adventure under way."

"May the Lord be with you two."

The pair left Father Jim's study and headed for the car park, winding their way through the concrete bunker-like corridors of dimmed recessed lighting and passing more of the same gray-clad personnel.

"So this Sasha, fella..." Ford said as they hustled through the hallway. "He really did it, discovered time travel?"

Alexander nodded, his mind too muddled to offer a reply as he contemplated the gravity of what he'd just signed up for again.

"And you did it, went back in time using his gizmo?"

"Yep," he simply said, his mind now working out how he was going to convince his friend to help him again after the trial run.

"Well, I'll be. Something straight out of Doctor Who, I reckon."

"Sure is." Though Alexander was sure Sasha would be livid comparing him to the fictional Britannia character from last century.

His mouth curled upward at the thought. He looked forward to seeing his college roommate again, the two basically having grown into young adulthood together through their mutual university and graduate studies. He hadn't heard from the man since returning to his parish before it all went down—literally. Figured the guy was wrapped up with his research, checking and crosschecking a million data points from his journey through the space-time continuum. He just hoped he was ready for round two.

They rounded a bend that would take them to the doors to the car park—

When they plowed into someone in a hurry, sending all three to the floor tripping over one another.

"Oof." "Ouch." "Hey!"

It was Tara Rodriguez.

Her eyes narrowed, and she huffed in irritation. "Watch it, would you, twinkle toes—times two."

Alexander glanced at Ford, who motioned with his head toward the lady and made a face that said all that needed to be said about the matter.

Father Jim wanted proof? Alexander would give him what he was certain he saw.

Now or never.

Tara went to stand—and that's when the two made their move, nodding at one another in agreement.

Alexander scrambled to Tara's back as she started rising, grabbing both arms from behind and yanking her back to the floor.

"What the..." she said with mystified disbelief. She craned her head back toward him and strained forward, but it was no use against his grip.

Ford grabbed Tara's wrist and peeled back one of her shirt-sleeves, searching for the offending mark that would offer the indictment he was looking for.

Not that one. He searched the underarm of her other sleeve as the woman shouted in protest and struggled to free herself.

There it was, plain as day.

A tattoo with two intersecting lines.

With one important detail missing.

The ends were not bent like Alexander had expected.

It was a tattoo, alright.

But of a Christian cross.

Definitely not the pagan-like symbol of the Church's archenemy.

Alexander immediately let go and scrambled backward, releasing her as if she were a python ready to strike. And rightly so, given the assault she had just endured.

"*Qué demonios estás haciendo!*" she shouted, yanking her arm back and shoving her sleeve back into place.

Ford's eyes went wide with surprise before his face fell and went white with mortification.

"I...uhh," he stammered. "We...uhh," he gestured to Alexander.

"I'll say it again," she said after bolting to her feet. "What the hell are you doing?"

"It's my fault," Alexander quickly said.

She spun around to face him, folding her arms and staring him down with those deep, penetrating Latin eyes. "Explain," she commanded.

He gulped down a lungful of air, then pointed and said, "The tattoo."

"The tattoo?"

Alexander took another breath, the color in his own face draining to white. He rubbed the back of his neck, then explained, "I saw it, on the underside of your wrist. And, well..."

"Spit it out, noob."

"I saw something similar on another person's arm a few days ago. Right after they ran into me coming down the path before my parish exploded."

"And, what, you thought that person was me?"

"No! Not at all," he said, trying to recover from a wicked-bad case of mistaken identity.

She widened her stance, continuing to stare him down. "Then what, pray tell?"

Alexander went to answer but couldn't spit it out.

Ford took over. "He thought it was the same markings of an

ancient enemy of the Church that has worked to undermine the faith."

Tara lowered her arms and spun around back to Ford. "What enemy? What gibberish are you talking about?"

He held up a hand. "Sorry, but that's classified."

Apparently the man had fully recovered his bravado. Alexander was mildly impressed but took a step back to avoid the anticipated eruption.

And it came.

Tara gasped, mouth open in appall and taking a dramatic step back before folding her arms again. "*Ca-lass-ified?* Are you joking? You assault me over some lame mistaken identity crazy-talk nonsense and then you have the gall to say the explanation behind it all is *classified?*"

Ford took a stabilizing breath, then widened his stance and folded his own arms. "Like I said, sorry ma'am. For the mistaken identity and all, as you put it. But, yes. Terribly sorry for the confusion."

Shaking her head, she said, "And you're the new head of operations. Of course! You know I applied for your job, right?"

Ford shrugged and said nothing.

She shook her head again. "Well, I'm sure glad we got it all cleared up that I'm not an enemy of Ichthus, working with the Church's historic nemesis to undermine and destroy the faith."

She said something in her native tongue again before brushing past him and disappearing beyond the corner, leaving the two men in her dust.

"Brutal," Alexander said.

Ford sighed, his color starting to return. "She was madder than a wet hen, I'd reckon."

"You think?" He came up beside the head of operations and added, "She raises the back of my neck hairs, that one does."

"You're telling me."

Alexander turned toward the frosted glass doors up ahead that led to the car park. "We should get going."

Ford nodded and started toward the doors. "Let's just hope that little encounter ain't an omen of things to come."

THUNDER RUMBLED in the distance above a thick canopy of dark billowing clouds as the AI cabbie came to a halting stop before a cluster of buildings that made up the Faculty of Physics of the University of Kiev. All drab, concrete functional slabs with no character or creativity still standing from the Soviet occupation, mausoleums of a dark period in Vostokana when totalitarianism reigned—reminding Solterra what was in store if citizens of the Republic weren't careful.

Alexander and Ford had hustled out from the Ministerium's headquarters after the embarrassing run-in with Tara. They caught the last magnarail headed for the third largest city in the pan-European continent and the anchoring capital of the Republic province in Vostokana. A few hours later, they were climbing into a rumbling cab driven by an AI humanoid that reminded Alexander of the one he had taken from Byzantium to Nicaea. Blessedly, the internal programming was different. He couldn't handle yet another random rendezvous. Although, knowing the good Lord had their back with such winks of providence offered a modicum of relief for their crazy adventure.

Ford paid the fare and off the humanoid went, leaving them to sort through the array of buildings and find their friend.

Another rumble of thunder coursed through the clouds above, sounding closer, more ominous, darkening the waning evening light and snapping the lampposts on to a golden LED hue that lined the concrete quad leading to the academic buildings.

"So where to now?" Ford asked Alexander, hands on his hips and eyeing each of the drab, utilitarian temples of higher academic learning. The emerging darkness made the angular accents of the buildings that much more dramatic.

Alexander pointed to a large, squat building at the center of a cluster of taller ones. "It's that building over there." A large raindrop slapped his forehead and slid down his face. He wiped it and said, "And we best get moving before this storm rolls in."

"You really think he's in there?" Ford replied as they hustled through a canopy of trees overhanging the sidewalk. "Just working into the wee hours of the evening on a Friday night?"

Alexander eyed the concrete monstrosity of utilitarian totalitarianism as they neared the building, searching for any sign of life of his former university roommate.

He smiled and pointed at the third floor. "Look, there." A golden hue shone with pride through a curtained window. Sasha's study. "He's there, alright."

"Then let's crash his lame-ass party," Ford said, pushing through the double doors that led into a vestibule.

The entryway ran high several stories, with elevators at one end and a wide metal staircase taking students and visitors up to the lecture halls and professor offices. An information desk commanded the center where Alexander recalled Father Jim breaking out his Muscovia language that dominated the Vostokana region of the former Eastern European nations that had been under the might and sway of former Russia to sweet talk a coed into Sasha's office. There was a slate device with what looked like an academic e-book for some university class on display, some snack wrappers, and a can of Coke. No one else was around. The rest of the space was dead, which made sense, given the end of the class week.

Ford spread his hands on the desk and sighed. Looking around, he said, "Must have gone to take a leak. But you know where to go, right?"

Alexander hesitated, feeling like they should wait for the missing attendant. But he nodded. "Yeah, third floor."

"Then up we go."

Ford led them up the central staircase, taking the stairs by two. At the top, he held out his arm for Alexander to take the lead.

He obliged, leading them down a long, vaulted hallway of the same utilitarian concrete. It was darker than the rest of the building, the lights having been turned down for the weekend. A faint glow at the end offered the only light, presumably coming from Sasha's office.

They reached the end of the corridor, finding a placard that announced the office of Dr. Sasha Pavlovich.

And the door was slightly ajar.

Alexander went to push through when a crash sounded forth from deep within.

He froze, stopping short and glancing at Ford. He continued forward, taking a cautious step inside. "Sash—"

Ford put his arm in the way of his advance and pushed him back into the hallway, bringing a finger up to his mouth to silence him. Alexander quickly stepped back.

Ford withdrew a weapon at his back from beneath his shirt and aimed it with a steady hand at the gap in the doorway.

"Where'd you get that?" Alexander hissed, taken aback by the presence of the firearm.

Ford shrugged. "From the Ministerium armory. Sig Sauer P365. Perfect balance of concealment and shootability."

"The Ministerium has an armory?"

"Uh, yeah. Filled with all the goodies of the Armor of God Saint Paul speaks of." He turned back, offering a wry grin.

Another crash echoed back through the gap and into the hallway.

Ford jerked toward the door and adjusted his grip. Without saying more, he motioned for Alexander to step back as he inched forward. He trained his weapon on the opening, then stepped forward to ease it open with his free hand. Another crash sounded deep inside as if in response, but Ford didn't startle this time.

Cool and steady, he put a foot inside the gap, then shoved through with extended weapon.

Alexander couldn't see anything past the man as he pressed farther inside the laboratory that sat before Sasha's well-appointed study in the back.

A second later, the ex-Solterra soldier suddenly yelled, "On the ground! On the ground!"

He sucked in a worried breath. *What the heck is going on?* Then he pressed forward himself.

Lord Jesus Christ, Son of God, Sasha better be safe!

That's when someone darted from the shadows out of view just past the threshold of the door inside, coming down hard on Ford's head with both arms. A body clad in black and face masked with the same hidden intent.

Ford discharged his weapon with a deafening blow in response. Another shot flashed and banged loudly, echoing down the corridor, exploding in the wall behind Alexander's shoulder.

He stopped short and pressed against the wall around the

door in the hallway, panic filling his mind and sending his gut to the floor.

This can't be happening...

Alexander closed his eyes and heaved several breaths as the melee continued around the corner inside the doorway. Then he snapped his eyes open and made a decision.

It was go time. Whether he wanted to or not.

On instinct, he offered a primal yell of anger, at both the turn of events and the man who had assaulted his comrade. He rounded the entrance and sprang upon the man to wrench him off from his partner.

The hostile was pure, hard muscle. And big, taller than Alexander himself. But he threw his arms around the man's neck and pulled with all his might.

The hostile let go, offering a choked yell as he flailed his thick arms in the air, batting at Alexander and throwing himself backwards. He crushed Alexander against a work table, sending instruments and a stack of books crashing to the floor.

But the priest maintained his hold, offering that primal yell again and tightening his grip.

Until the man threw his head back with a jerk, landing a painful blow straight into Alexander's nose.

Blood burst from the impact, a geyser of crimson running down his face.

He slouched against the table and slid to the floor, hitting it hard.

But not before Ford was able to lurch forward and recover from the original assault.

Just as a second figure appeared deeper inside a second room that made up Sasha's study, silhouetted by the glow of the room. He raised his arms, looking as if he was taking aim to bring the invasion to a decisive close.

A *pop-pop-pop* echoed back to Alexander.

He flinched on instinct, crouching and shielding his face. When he chanced a look, the man had fallen and Ford was running toward him, weapon extended.

The man who had assaulted Ford from the shadows recovered, scrambling off the ground and hustling toward the exit as Ford reached the man he had just shot.

Alexander was paralyzed from the violence of it all to do anything about his escape.

The hostile darted out into the hallway, his footfalls echoing toward the stairs and away to safety.

Another *pop-pop* startled Alexander. He whipped his head toward his partner and sat up on his knees for a look. Ford was standing over the man, aiming for his head. He'd shot him point-blank.

Heaving heavy breaths, he scrambled toward his partner just inside the study. "What did you do?"

Ford turned to him, his face a mixture of steely confidence and confused irritation.

"Saved our backsides, that's what."

"Shouldn't we have taken him into custody or something?"

Ford scoffed and shoved the weapon at his back. "That dude wasn't going into any custody, I can tell you that."

Alexander stared at the man, two holes blown in his head and blood pooling at the back. He closed his eyes and took in a breath. A burning bile feeling worked its way up his throat and threatened to burst. He averted his eyes, scanning the study in search of any sign of his friend and taking in the wicked sight.

Books printed before the Reckoning were scattered about. Lamps were smashed to the floor, their shades tattered. Drawers from Sasha's wooden desk that commanded one end of the vast space were toppled about. The overstuffed chairs and couch that he and Father Jim and Sasha had sat in just days ago, arguing about time travel and leveraging the man's discovery for Ichthus, were slit and torn, their white stuffing pluming like a foaming mouth.

Hostiles had ransacked Sasha Pavlovich's university study.

But why?

Was it a botched robbery gone bad, the thieves not expecting the man to be there late on a Friday night? Or the mob, perhaps, people he owed money coming to collect?

Then it hit him.

The time travel device.

He heard a whistle. Ford, motioning for him to take a look at the floor.

Alexander looked down to see the man kneeling next to his prize, the slain hostile. He was holding his arm, having pushed the man's sleeve up from his wrist.

"Is this here the bird tattoo you were referring to earlier?"

Alexander's mouth went dry; his bowels went weak.

Yes, it was.

He swallowed and quickly nodded.

Ford huffed, then cursed. Then he voiced what they already knew: "Nous..."

Alexander said nothing, staring in disbelief at the arm that bore the same intersecting lines bent at odd angles echoing a wicked, totalitarian menace that had plagued the world before through a world war, and inspiring the persecution and destruction of the Church for two millennia.

"Well, that's a fine kettle of fish we just walked into. I've gotta call this in. Cardinal Ferraro's gonna have a conniption if—"

A moan from the corner, behind an overturned table, caught both of their attention. They looked at each other, recognition hitting them.

Alexander was the first to hustle toward the sound. "Sasha?" he yelled.

Another moan, more movement.

He reached the table and lifted it back.

Discovering a very beat-up Sasha Pavlovich beneath it.

"My God…"

"Hold up there, partner," Ford said, kneeling next to the man whose face was darkening with blotchy spots from clear bruising. "You took quite a beating. Let's make sure nothing is—"

Sasha yelled, interrupting the man's triage.

"Broken." He motioned toward Alexander. "Help me get rid of this debris, will ya?"

The two moved the overturned table that had been stacked with books and devices and other odds-and-ends and cleared away the debris that had fallen over Sasha.

"Help me move him into a better position," Ford said, grabbing Sasha's upper body while Alexander grabbed his feet. "Now, gentle…."

Sasha grabbed for his arm, bent at an ungodly angle, as they moved him into a stabilizing position.

"Sit tight, partner. We'll get you patched up in no time."

Ford stood and started scoping around the space.

Alexander took in several worried breaths kneeling next to his friend and feeling utterly helpless. "Sasha, brother, what in the world happened here?"

"They came for it?"

"For what?"

"The device."

So it *was* about the time travel.

"Who came for it?"

Sasha screamed again, his face twisting with pain. He took in quick breaths, as if he were in labor, then gritted his teeth again.

Alexander looked away, unable to handle the sight of his friend in such agony.

Ford returned, bearing a broken piece of wood and some shredded cloth.

"Alright, partner. I'm going to check out your arm and see what's going on with the thing. Then I'm going to set it. Got it?"

Sasha looked at him with wide moist eyes, then nodded his understanding.

Ford didn't waste any time. He first probed the rest of his body. Sasha moaned with displeasure, but the man was satisfied the professor wasn't damaged elsewhere. Then he gently probed the arm resting limp on the man's chest at a wicked angle at the elbow.

That's when Sasha screamed again and slugged Ford with his other arm.

He shielded himself from the man's blows and chuckled. "At least we know the other arm still works."

"That's the Sasha I know," Alexander said.

"Why don't you try being attacked by terrifying terrorists and beaten to a pulp!" Sasha moaned. "And now it's being all tingly!"

Ford said, "Looks like the arm ain't broke. Just dislocated."

"Just dislocated?" Sasha yelled.

He nodded toward Alexander. "Hold him down while I..."

Alexander understood and shuffled around to his friend's head.

Sasha looked from him to Ford. "What is happening? What is it you are doing?"

"Just hold still, Sasha. You've got this."

"Got what?"

Ford gently took the arm, while Alexander held Sasha's shoulders in position.

"On three," the man said.

"What three? What is it you are talking about?" asked Sasha, his voice laced with delirium.

"One, two—"

There was a crunch as Ford yanked on Sasha's arm and slid it back into place, followed by a momentary silence, as if time hung in between two sets of pain.

Then agonizing cries roared to life.

"Just be thankful it ain't broke, ya big baby," Ford mumbled as he stood.

"I no big baby!" Sasha moaned, joining the man. "Now, get me a tall glass of Ukrainski candy."

Alexander wrapped an arm around his friend's shoulder and gave it a tug. "Glad you're alive, friend. Those blokes meant serious business."

"You're telling me," he said as he shuffled over to a minibar nestled between two bookcases. He grabbed a bottle of vodka and a double-size tumbler, then poured with abandon four-fingers worth, no ice.

Leaning against the minibar, Sasha threw back a mouthful and sighed with pleasure, a grin spreading across his face. He took a step toward his friends, but faltered, stumbling against Ford and sloshing some of his vodka over the man.

"Whoa there, fella." Ford slung an arm around Sasha's back and helped him forward.

"I'd ask you to make yourself comfortable, but..." Sasha eyed the overturned study. "Look at the place!" He took another long swig as Ford helped him to the couch.

He gave a choking screech and started launching a string of words in the Muscovia tongue, pointing to the floor near the arrangement of couches and chairs.

The dead Nous hostile.

Ford looked to Alexander, then said, "Yeah, about that..."

CHAPTER 13

Alexander pushed the stuffing back into place in the couch as Sasha continued babbling with delirious confusion in the tongue of his homeland, clearly freaked at the sight of the dead man bleeding out on his study floor. Probably also a delayed response from the trauma of the evening. Who could blame him?

A part of him wanted to join in the babbling, his stomach churning after glancing down at the masked figure lying prone on the woven rug. He had never seen a dead body before, let alone someone shot. Probably wouldn't be the last time, now that he was following Ford around. And now it seemed like the norm for the Ministerium itself, given what Ichthus was now up against.

Ford and Sasha reached the couch. He helped ease the professor down to recuperate. Alexander and his partner took up the other abused overstuffed chairs bleeding their stuffing, pushing it back inside and clearing some of it away.

Sasha settled in and threw back another mouthful of Ukrainski candy, draining the glass. He held it out with his good arm. "Be a good boy, Alex, and get me some more vodka, please?"

Alexander smiled and took it, then headed back to the minibar. "Rocks or straight?" he asked holding up the glass and the bottle of Stolichnaya.

"Ice this time. Should still be some left in the bucket from earlier. My head is pounding, and a cold glass will be doing it some good, methinks." Wincing as he adjusted his position, he added, "Now who the hell was that dead man over there all bleeding out on my study floor?"

Ford glanced at Alexander as he walked over with Sasha's drink. He cleared his throat and answered, "He was part of a two-man team we think was part of a clandestine organization that wants to hurt Ichthus."

Sasha grabbed the glass and promptly took a drink, humming with pleasure. He brought the glass to his head, wincing again, and asked, "And who the hell are you being?"

"This is my new...partner, I guess," Alexander said, slumping back in his chair. "John Mark Ford. Ex-Legion and head of Ministerium security operations."

Ford threw him a look at the mention of the Solterra military and shook his head. Wrong move.

"Ex-Legion?" Sasha questioned, eyes closed and hand rocking the tumbler back and forth against his head. "There is being no *ex*-Solterra military, from my understanding. You either military or you not. No ex about it. Which means you must be being a deserter or something. Which means there be a big fat bounty for your head, Legion."

Ford shifted in his seat and crossed his legs, his face registering annoyance at the man's questioning. "Yes, well. Things didn't turn out the way I had hoped. So sue me. Or, turn me in if you're itchin' for a good lynchin'."

"Perhaps Sasha will do just that. Cash in and retire to a life of Stoli and *devochki*."

Alexander chuckled. "I don't think you'd sit still long

enough to enjoy a life of vodka and young women, Sasha. And besides, he's with me. You mess with him, you mess with me. Got it?"

Sasha groaned and waved a dismissive hand, as if he understood. Ford took a breath and nodded his appreciation to Alexander.

"So, what happened?" the priest asked gently, leaning toward his friend to scope for answers.

"What the hell you be thinking happened?" Sasha replied, waving his glass around with a more-than-normal amount of crankiness. Which Alexander understood, given the circumstances.

"Look, Sasha, we're just trying to understand what happened here. One man jumped Ford, and then we had it out before he fled. The other...Well, you know what happened to him. Then we find your place trashed, and you moaning and groaning under an overturned table..."

"Botched robbery," Sasha said, returning the glass to his head. "That is what happened."

"This was more than a simple robbery. I mean, look at this place! They turned it inside out, clearly looking for something." He hesitated, then added, "You said the device was safe. That they didn't get it."

Alexander paused, searching his friend's face. Then he said lowly, "They wanted it, didn't they, the time travel device?"

Sasha scoffed. "I said simple robbery. That is all that this was being. I was working. The men came in. Probably after seeing the stupid report on OneWorld News, which I knew I never should have been doing for precisely this reason. And, yes, they demand time travel device. Probably to go joyriding or something. Or sell it on the black market."

"Yeah, that's not who this was," Ford said bluntly. "And that's not what happened here."

"Really, smarty pants? Then what was this being?"

Ford took a breath. "As I said before, the man on the floor was part of an organization called Nous. An occult-like, alt-spiritual group that's been battling Ichthus for two millennia. A tattoo marking on the underside of the arm of the dead dude was the clear giveaway."

Sasha took a long swig of his vodka, then returned the glass to his head, mumbling, "And here I thought it was Solterra's fault."

"Solterra?" he asked, leaning forward. "Why's that?"

"Because right before the one muscle head ripped my arm out of its socket, he be saying that me handing over the device was *'For Humanity.'*"

"For Humanity?"

"*Da.* For Humanity. For Humanity! He just kept repeating that creepy phrase of the Republic. Stood the hairs up all over my arms, he did. Right before the man was snapping it out of joint."

Ford looked at Alexander, his face etched with the same dread that started winding its way through Alexander. If Solterra was involved in the heist attempt on top of Nous...well that turned this whole thing into a whole other thing.

"Wait a minute..." Sasha said. "Why you two here?"

"What?" Alexander replied, caught off guard in his contemplation.

The professor eased himself upright and finished his vodka. He waved his empty glass at Ford and then at Alexander. "I didn't know you be coming here tonight. Don't get me wrong. I am being grateful you showed up unannounced and all."

"You're welcome for that, by the way," Ford said with an edge. Couldn't blame him, given Sasha's crankiness. But neither the time nor the place to poke the cranky beast.

Sasha ignored him and cast a skeptical eye on Alexander.

"So why you show up here tonight? If it is being about the very same time travel device that Solterra or this Nous organization, whatever the hell that is…I'm not being happy, Alex."

Alexander said nothing, folding his hands together on his lap and looking at the floor.

"*Nyet!*"

"Come on, Sasha. We need your help!"

"*Nyet, nyet, nyet!*" the professor said, shooting up from the couch. Then he cried out in pain and collapsed, sinking back into the damaged upholstery and holding his empty tumbler out again. "I think I am going to be needing another one of these. And this time, no ice."

⸻

THUNDER CONTINUED ROLLING ABOVE THE OFFICE complex in menacing bursts, joined by lashing rain continuing its assault on the windows. Alexander flinched at another outburst as he brought back a third round of vodka, sans ice. Then he began filling Sasha in on what had happened the past few days.

He began with running into the purported Nous terrorist before the terrorism that assaulted his parish brought the building to its knees—and his people to early graves.

"This is being crazy talk!" he said, jolting up again with only a slight wince now, the Ukrainski candy clearly working its magic. He swallowed another mouthful. "I heard about some church being bombed to smithereens, but I was having no idea it was being yours, Alex."

"What's even crazier talk is that I'm pretty sure the same tattoo marking that was on the underside of that dead guy lying over there on your study floor was also on the wrist of the person I saw running away from my parish."

"That is being even crazier crazy talk!"

Alexander frowned. "You're telling me."

Sasha took another swig and shook his head. "So you're saying Solterra bombed your parish?"

"Nous," Ford said.

He sighed and leaned back against the couch. "I am not being able to keep all of this straight."

Alexander chuckled. "I hear you. But there's more. Do you remember my ministry friend Father Josiah Abasi?"

"Hmm," Sasha hummed. "Not really."

"It's OK, doesn't matter. But he recently defected to Panligo, and then he spouted all of this...crazy talk, as you say, about God and spirituality and the need for some sort of next iteration of religion."

"Sounds like my kind of guy," he mumbled before taking another swig.

"Well, he's not," Alexander snapped. "Because he's basically declared war on Ichthus. And..."

He took a breath before getting to the reason for them being there. "And Father Jim wants us to search for a lost Order that might help us in the fight."

Sasha drained his vodka. "A lost Order? Like Freemasons or something?"

Alexander shook his head. "It's called the Order of Thaddeus. Throughout the Church's history, they've helped sort of protect Ichthus and her faith."

"Like the jihadis of Muhammedism?"

"Not exactly. At any rate, they've gone into hiding and Father Jim thinks we can leverage your time travel device to find some sort of clue that could lead to their whereabouts."

"That man needs a new hobby, methinks," Sasha said.

Alexander chuckled. "I hear you. Not too keen on the idea myself, going back—" He sighed and shook his head at the idea. "Back in time again. And I know how big of an ask it is..."

Sasha said nothing. His eyes were closed, and he was spinning his empty tumbler in his hand.

He finally said, "How is it you are asking this of me after what I just went through? I gave in the first time as a personal favor. And then I trusted you the first time to be keeping me safe. But look at what happened!"

He waved the arm holding the tumbler around the room, settling in the direction of the body still lying on the floor.

"I almost died tonight!" Sasha exclaimed. "I was thinking maybe thieves were trying to swipe my invention after seeing the news on OneWorld. But now I am finding out it was religious zealots warring against Ichthus. Connected in some way to the Ministerium who was supposed to have kept me safe, is that right?"

He had a point. Father Jim had promised him that the full resources of the Ministerium would protect him after offering his device to send Alexander back in time. Not their fault he balked at their suggestions to go underground into the arms of their protective custody. Couldn't dream of leaving behind his research and prestigious career at the university.

But still...the man had indeed been almost killed. And quite possibly for offering aid and comfort to the Church.

Alexander looked to Ford, who shrugged, then went to say more when Sasha interrupted.

"I'll agree to this second little trip, but only on one condition. Well, two."

He flashed a hopeful smile at his partner and sat to the edge of his chair. "Anything. Whatever you want to help further your research, I'm in."

"First, you better be protecting me for real after this time. For really real this time."

"Done. But that means you need to follow orders and take the hand Father Jim offered. Can you ensure the Ministerium can keep him safe, Ford?"

"Absolutely. If he follows my orders," Ford said.

Sasha sighed and nodded.

"What's the second thing?" asked Alexander.

The man sat up and scooted to the middle of the couch. Folding his legs under himself, he said, "And second, not just you. Both."

Now Ford himself sat up straight and scooted to the edge of his chair. "Uh, come again, partner? Both what?"

"Both, both. You both go."

"Back in time?" he exclaimed, flashing Alexander a panicked look.

"Yessiree."

"I don't think that's a good idea—"

"It's my final offer," Sasha said, waving his hand in the air dismissively.

"How can you even do that?" Alexander asked. "Last I remember, the traveler had to slap on some sort of radioactive belt around their waist. Which didn't at all look big enough for two."

"Wait a minute. Radioactive belt?" Ford questioned, swallowing hard at the idea.

Alexander suppressed a grin, reveling at the loss of confidence in the guy who exuded way too much bravado for his liking.

"Yes, you are being correct," Sasha said, a knowing look playing across his face. "The one belt is not being big enough for you both..."

Then it hit Alexander. His eyes went wide with recognition and he stood.

"You've got another one, don't you?" he whispered, as if

Solterra itself would hear the bombshell reveal and come barging back inside to take it.

Sasha said nothing, simply smiling his affirmation.

Ford sighed and slid back into his chair. "That's crazier than a dog in a cat factory."

CHAPTER 14

Lightning flashed a staccato rhythm of white, followed quickly by a bang of thunder. The three jumped at the sound as the storm assaulted the building directly overhead. Rain lashed angrily against the windows now, a refrain that offered a soundtrack as Sasha hobbled over to the minibar.

Ford looked at Alexander in confusion. "Pretty soon, this guy's skin is gonna start bleeding vodka if we don't put a pacer on his consumption."

"He's not going for more alcohol," Alexander said. "Come on."

He walked to join Sasha just as he pressed the button to unlock the hidden room behind the study. A *shi-cuh* sounded as the pressurized door engaged, and the minibar began to sink into the adjoining hidden room, disappearing behind the wall.

Ford joined them. "Apparently our terrorist guests didn't know about the bat cave hidden behind the minibar."

"Apparently not," Alexander said. "And thank the good Lord above they didn't." Although he had to imagine Sasha would have taken less of a beating had they known.

Sasha motioned for them to join him. He led them inside the darkened space. "Lights, turn on," he commanded.

The room lit to a dull whitish-blue hue. A table of glass and chrome commanded the center with a large rack server blinking like a Christmas tree sitting in the far corner. A series of four workstations were connected to it by snaking thick cords along the wall.

And in the center of the table was what Alexander and Ford had travelled to Kiev for—literally risking life and limb, given the raid by the Nous hostiles.

Not one, but two electromagnetic time travel devices.

They looked like oversized chocolate donuts, with four more donut-like rings sitting at each of the four edges at ninety-degree intervals.

Ford walked to the table and whistled, picking up a belt. "Well, I'll be. This here donut's some fine sci-fi engineering you got, doc. All H. G. Wells and stuff, eh?"

Sasha took it back and carefully set it on the table, then sat on a stool at his worktable. "I am not knowing about no Wells. But it is fine Vostokanan engineering for sure."

Oh, Sasha. Ever the nationalist.

"You didn't say anything about *two* belts a week ago when Father Jim and I dropped by," Alexander said.

Sasha shrugged. "I thought it best to see if one belt worked first."

"You mean, to see if I came back alive instead of dragging both of your time travel belts with me to Lord knew where?"

Sasha said nothing.

"Break it down, doc," Ford said. "What's this doodad do?"

"Several centuries ago, someone named Frank Wilczek—"

"Skip the history lesson, prof," he interrupted. "Just give it to me straight."

"I'm getting there, Legion. Now if you wouldn't be interrupting..."

Ford crossed his arms and motioned for him to continue.

"Anyway, let me share an illustration that is more your speed. Most people think of objects as having length, width, and height, right?"

He took a book sitting on a counter behind him and placed it in front of the two men, tracing the sides of the book to illustrate length and width, then edging the spine with his finger to illustrate height.

Alexander recalled the illustration from before. It was a good one, and Ford seemed to be getting into it.

"But what most people don't realize is that the book also occupies a place in time I call *phasement.*"

He lifted the book upward and traced an imaginary line downward.

"Which means you can travel along this line down into time. At one point this book was in the bookshelf, that's one phase. Then it was placed on the counter behind me before I brought it to the table, two more phases in time. The fourth dimension sort of records this placement along time in the past, just like the x, y, z dimensions record its occupancy of space in the present."

"OK..." Ford said, looking at Alexander who smiled in amusement. "But what the hey-ho day does this matter for us here and now? What of this belt nonsense?"

Sasha rolled his eyes. "To test his theory, Professor Wilczek used an electromagnetic field to demonstrate that the translational symmetry of time could be broken. He failed. But a few years later, a team of physicists from UC Berkeley verified his theories, discovering a new phase of matter and verifying his previous hypothesis."

"Time crystals," Alexander said, "if I recall."

"*Da.* Time crystals. Solid, liquid, gas weren't the only kids on the physics block anymore. Now there was this new phase of matter called the time crystal."

"And what is a...a time crystal?" asked Ford.

"A totally new state of matter whose atomic structure repeats through time as regular matter repeats in space—or even changes, which is where things get remarkable."

"Come again?"

Sasha explained, "Take water. At its normal state, it's a liquid. Add energy to it, and you have steam. Reduce the amount of potential energy, you are having solid ice. So three states of matter and its placement in space. But Wilczek theorized that if you could move the atoms from their original position in some way, then it would break time-translation symmetry and transform its *phasement* as well."

"My head is hurting..." Ford complained.

"Come on, Legion, stay with me," Sasha huffed. "OK, fine. Try this. Imagine three people playing jump rope: Alexander and me are holding a rope while you jump in the middle."

"Hated jump rope as a kid."

"You and me both," Alexander said.

Sasha continued, "So, Alex, you and me, our arms make a full rotation every two seconds."

"That seems too fast for my liking," Ford complained. "What about three?"

"No! Two seconds. That two-second motion sets the time-translation symmetry, where the period of time the rope comes around again is two seconds, like clockwork. But what would happen if our arms rotated four or five times, but the rope only made one rotation?"

"I would have to jump only once?"

"Well, yes."

Alexander added, "And the time-translation symmetry would be broken. Since our motion rotating the rope would be out of sync with Ford's motion of jumping—in essence, two separate phases of time."

"*Da*! Sounds like our late-night debates back at Oxford weren't an entire waste, Alex," Sasha said. "You be catching on quick."

"And the time crystal breaks this?" asked Ford. "Both in space and in time?"

"*Da.* The researchers in California found that time crystals can break the time-translation symmetry over a period of time through the creation of an electromagnetic field and the addition of laser pulses. They were able to alter the phase of ions through time—revolutionizing how we perceive matter existing in time as it exists in space. The only problem, is that there was little practical application for the new phase of matter."

Alexander added, "Until now..."

Sasha smiled knowingly. "The technology finally got small enough where I could harness it all into these belts. Which required combining the insights of a few more theoretical physicists. Stephen Hawking and Michio Kaku, two brilliant minds who explored the depths of quantum physics and string theory, recognized one could warp the space-time continuum to create a sort of bridge by focusing highly energized laser beams on the pockets of hydrogen-rich lithium deuteride contained inside the device, incinerating the material and creating a mini explosion—"

"Mini explosion?" Ford interrupted.

"*Da.* But not to worry. It is totally contained within a graphite shield. The explosion releases a fusion reaction that unleashes enough energy to open a wormhole in the space-time continuum."

"A wormhole? Is this guy for real?" Ford said to Alexander.

Alexander shrugged. "Worked for me. And he did beam a bunch of bunnies back in time."

"In past centuries," Sasha continued, "time was treated like a set of magnarail tracks—it was thought to have gone this way and that." He moved his hand across his forearm, from his elbow to the end of his hand, then back again. "But some began to wonder whether there were loops and branches along the way that could bring the choo-choo back again to a station it had passed by earlier. It was after the mathematician Kurt Gödel discovered a new space-time allowed by general relativity that we could posit warping local regions of the continuum to allow time travel. That, combined with the theory of relativity that implies you can travel back in time if you can travel faster than the speed of light, brought the science fiction into science fact."

"That sounds about as safe as a helicopter with an ejection seat," Ford said. "But how does this doohickey work this voodoo magic?"

"The electromagnetic field. This not only transforms the matter of the host into a new phase of matter that transcends the continuum, but also envelops them inside the warped region of the continuum, the wormhole—a thin tube of space-time that flattens the phases of history into a next-door region you can just zip into through to the other side."

"Now that's nutty. But how do you jump us into the right phase of time, Mr. Spock?"

"An on-board computer," Sasha explained, "uses a highly sophisticated algorithm to create a localized wormhole, warping the local region of the space-time continuum by focusing the energy stored in the belt onto a single point. This not only transforms the matter of the host into a new phase of matter that transcends the continuum. It also envelops them inside the warped region of the continuum, the wormhole—a thin tube of space-time that flattens the phases of history into a next-door region you can just zip into the precise phasement. Like folding a piece of paper and punching a hole through the center, bringing the two dots from two locations along the plane of the paper into one single phase."

Ford folded his arms. "What about the return trip home?"

"All the energy necessary for both the trip through time and back is stored in the belt through the hydrogen fusion process. The beauty is that by combining these two aspects of theoretical physics—time crystals of matter and warping space-time—I was able to open a doorway into the past that allows physical matter to jump phases."

"Like those bunnies you beamed out of here?"

"*Da.*"

"What about us humans?"

"The only reason they didn't come back is because they weren't wearing the belt. Only standing in a little box. But the good thing is they didn't vaporize into a pile of goop!"

"That you know of."

Sasha shrugged. "Like Alexander said, he came back without incident."

"Well, is it safe?" Ford said, turning to Alexander.

"Not if you expect to have any children," Sasha deadpanned.

Ford glanced down at his crotch, widening his eyes.

"Kidding! It's all very contained and very safe. The beauty is that there is little waste material generated in the process of generating the power around the belt between the four poles. Barely any radiation is emitted. Not more than your Solterra-issued mobile."

A silence settled over the room. Ford brought a hand to his chin and stroked it in contemplation. Alexander looked on, as did Sasha.

"Alright," Ford finally said. "This sounds crazier than... well, the craziest thing I could think of thinking. But I'm satisfied."

Alexander grinned and glanced at Sasha with a nod.

"But now what's this?" Ford reached for a cap that had been resting on the table next to the donut belt. He scrunched up his face as he looked at the smooth black oval device.

"A neural core sensory receptor," Sasha said.

He stared at the man, eyes unblinking with confusion. "Come again, doc?"

Sasha rolled his eyes. "It retrieves sensory data inputted through your experience, a sort of net that gathers the sound and sight information from your brain waves, sending them to a memory unit on board. Sort of like old-school Google Glass headset, but it uses your brain waves to record the information entering your neural core and then a powerful AI algorithm translates that neural data into images and sound."

Ford whistled. "Now that's legit sci-fi shiznit right there. You're like Batman or something, aren't you? A gadget for everything."

"With this attachment," Alexander said, taking the black cap device and holding it up, "we can record the entire experience using our own brainwave activity from our eyes and ears. It's how we captured my conversation with John the apostle."

"Y'all have clearly lost your vertical hold on life," Ford mumbled, shaking his head and retrieving the device from Alexander.

"Excuse me?" Sasha said, looking at Alexander for a translation. He shrugged.

"You're telling me," Ford went on, "this here device receives transmissions from the brain and then processes that information from our eyes and ears, all light and audio waves received from the outside world? So, what, us time travelers can bring back our experience like some cinemamaker?"

"You've got it."

Ford whistled and shook his head as he rubbed his forehead. "My mind's turning to peanut butter over how nutty this all is."

Alexander chuckled. "I understand the feeling. Felt the same way when I first heard about it all. But I lived to tell about it. It works, man. It really works." He reached over to Sasha and squeezed his shoulder. "And all because of this genius here."

"Well, then. I guess we best get to it."

"Get to what?" asked Sasha, taking back the cap and bringing the time travel belt closer to himself.

"A parade down the Champs-Élysées in Francia. What do you think I mean? Time travel!"

The Ukrainski professor stood and leaned back against the counter, saying nothing.

"Sasha..." Alexander said.

He replied, "The vodka is now wearing off, and I am remembering all of what I went through to discover the final pieces of the puzzle to time travel. And then build the device to make it happen." Sasha went to fold his arms but winced, the memory of the dislocation also returning.

Alexander glanced at Ford, who gave him a look that told him to close the deal.

He stepped toward his friend and put his hand on his shoulder. "I understand, mate, I do. But think about all of the work you can do helping Ichthus—helping the world. Your research won't stop, not for a long shot." Alexander paused and chuckled. "In fact, you'd be surprised how technologically advanced the Church has become in the shadows of Solterra."

Sasha scoffed. "Now you be drunk on Ukrainski candy, methinks."

"I'm serious! Tell him, Ford."

"He's right," the man said. "I can't go into details here, but suffice it to say...you'll be adequately protected and equipped to continue your work."

Sasha took in a breath and held it, then rubbed his head. He exhaled it heavily and said, "And I'll have everything I need to continue my work?"

"Whatever you need," Alexander said.

The man closed his eyes and nodded.

Alexander slowly exhaled and shot Ford a glance, a grin playing across his face.

Thank the—

His rejoicing was cut short by his mobile phone vibrating in his pocket. He withdrew the device.

Father James Ferraro.

Answering, he said, "Father Jim. Was getting ready to—"

"It's happened," the cardinal interrupted.

"What's happened?"

"Panligo has let slip the dogs of war!"

CHAPTER 15

Alexander closed his eyes and sighed. *Now what.*

"Give it to us straight, chief," Ford said.

"Those damned Protestants have jumped ship!" Father Jim exclaimed.

"What are you talking about, Padre?" Alexander asked. "What have the Protestants done? Which ones?"

"The bloody lot of them, that's who! They've followed their leaders off the cliffs into heretical denial of historic Christian orthodoxy by joining with the lot of Cardinal Weiss and Bishop Nicolai and...well, Bishop Abasi. Completely jettisoning Ichthus in favor of the singular united religious assembly we've all come to know and love as—"

"Panligo," Ford said, finishing his announcement.

Father Jim simply nodded with a jolting scoff. "They've gone stark mad, the whole lot of them! Though not at all a surprise considering the direction Protestant Orthodoxy has been going in the past century, following the lead of Mainline Protestants from former Western nations."

That was crazy. And he was right: It was not surprising. But still. An entire wing of Ichthus gone? Separated from the Church?

"So you're suggesting that, what, just like that, the third largest tribe within Ichthus has just up and left?" asked Alexander.

"Not suggesting, lad. Telling!" exclaimed Father Jim. "I received word an hour ago that the major leaders within the faction of the Church had met in a conclave all their own. Irony of ironies, considering the stunt Weiss and Nicolai and the others pulled, infiltrating our own meeting of the minds and all. At any rate, they voted overwhelmingly to disaffect from Ichthus and join hands with Panligo. Our Asiatica and Alkebulana brothers and sisters staged a mighty fierce protest of disavowal, but to no avail. Rumor is, those leaders from the southern and eastern quarters of Solterra are attempting to disassociate from the faction, trying to keep their parish properties and ministries alive. However, all does not bode well for them, as the leaders from Europa and Americana and California and Cascadia carry not only the power of the purse but the imprimatur of Solterra as well, given their cozy relationship with the Republic. I fear for them. For their property, yes. But also, their very lives."

"Then I'd say we best get a move on," Ford said. "Sounds like our mission is even more crucial given the circumstances."

"Indeed. I presume you've rendezvoused with our good friend Dr. Pavlovich and secured his cooperation?" He bent his head this way and that, smiling and searching for the man.

Alexander nodded. "We did. Say 'Hello,' Sasha."

Sasha came into view and waved. "*Dobre dein*, Father Ferraro. Good to be seeing you again."

"Likewise, my boy!" Padre replied. "I trust you've been a good lad and offered your services with full cooperation."

Alexander chuckled and slapped Sasha on the back. "Took a bit of convincing, but he came around. Was nice enough to let us don the guinea pig costume again. Only, on one condition."

"Oh? And what was that?"

Ford glanced at Alexander. "That I saddle up and join the party."

"What? How is that possible?" asked Father Jim.

"Apparently, the man was holding out on you two."

"Sasha had developed two belts," Alexander explained. "Wanted to make sure I came back in one piece."

Padre laughed. "That Sasha's a clever little bugger, I'd say. More the merrier, I'd say. And safer, I'd imagine. Jolly well, off you go. Say hello to good ol' Saint Jude for me, will you?"

Alexander chuckled. "We will."

"Roger, roger, chief," Ford said. "But there was a bit of a wrinkle on the mission you probably should know about before we sign off."

"Good Lord. As if the abandonment of Ichthus by Protestant Orthodoxy wasn't enough..." the man mumbled. "What now?"

Ford took a breath. "Nous."

Father Jim said nothing, the connection appearing as though it had dropped.

The two looked at each other and then to the mobile device.

"Padre?" Alexander said. "You there?"

"Yes, lad. I'm still here," Father Jim said lowly, as if suddenly worried the Republic would be listening in.

"Nous, you say?"

Ford answered, "That's right. Two thugs intercepted the professor before we arrived. Tore up his laboratory and study. Ruffled up Doc Pavlovich pretty good, too."

Father Jim moaned and mumbled a curse under his breath. "And you're sure it was them?"

"Positive. I managed to, well, incapacitate one of the goons. The stick tattoo, the one Alexander described, the one of the rising phoenix he saw on the fella running from his parish and we thought we saw on Tara. It was right there on the hostile's wrist, plain as day."

"I'm sure I don't have to say so, but I'm guessing it appears the men were after the very object of desire we ourselves were?"

"Roger that."

"I shan't imagine this bodes well for Ichthus."

Ford frowned. "I shan't not, chief. If Nous is after the time travel device, then we've got a whole other kettle of fish to worry about. And Sasha mentioned one of the goons had asked that he give it up in service *'For Humanity'*."

"For Humanity?" Father Jim exclaimed.

"Yes."

"The plot thickens, with the apparent hand of Solterra churning the butter."

"Appears so. And I don't have to tell you how bad this looks to see Nous and the Republic in bed together."

Father Jim sighed. "Nothing good will come from their copulation."

"Vivid image, chief. But yes, we need to explore this further. Perhaps get Tara on the case in our absence."

"Ms. Rodriguez? But why, when she appears in cahoots with Nous?"

Ford looked to Alexander for cover. He offered it, saying, "Yeah, about that, Padre. It looks like I may have been mistaken about her."

"Oh? Do tell."

"We, shall we say, intercepted her before leaving for Kiev. And it looks like the tattoo was of a cross. An Ichthus cross, not some pagan, Nous impersonation."

"Good Lord! And good to know the Ministerium isn't

harboring the Devil in our midst. I'll smooth things over with her in your absence and we'll sort it all when you return."

"Thanks, chief," Ford said.

"Speaking of our absence," Alexander said. "Where do you suggest we go to find Jude Thaddeus? And perhaps the better question should be, when?"

"The apostle is one of the least understood," Father Jim said, "with some of the least background details available, either from the New Testament itself or from other extant sources from the era. We know he was martyred in the latter part of AD 65. And it seems he and his companion Simon the Zealot, as he was affectionately known, were stationed in Syria, probably in Beirut. If I were to venture a guess, I'd say that's as good as any place, and *phase,* to start with."

"Not a lot to go on, but I guess that's all we've got during these perilous times." Alexander glanced at Ford. "But what about your grasp of the *lingua franca* of the—"

"I can hold my own," Ford interrupted. "Took up Hebrew during my downtime with the Legion. Close enough to Aramaic, so I'll be fine."

"Alright then. I guess that settles it."

"May the Lord be with you two," said Father Jim.

Alexander offered an *Amen,* then he ended the call and stowed the mobile device back in his pocket.

"I suppose we should get a move on," Ford said. He turned to Sasha. "So what's up, doc? How do we strap into these things and ride off into time?"

"First things first," Sasha said, reaching for the small cap-like neural core device the size of his palm. He handed it to Alexander. "You be remembering this, don't you?"

"How could I forget?" Alexander said, recalling the way the neurotransmission device affected all of his sensory perception.

Sasha grabbed the cap from Alexander and placed it on his head, the familiar tentacles from underneath stretching outward to hold itself firmly to his skull. "Be remembering that it knows when you place it on your head and will grab on, so you don't have to worry about it coming loose. The button at the top releases it." He pressed the button, and it popped off like the jaw of an animal releasing its prey. "Like before, you should be wearing a hat or something, because it will be visible."

Sasha removed the device from Alexander's head, then took the belt off the table. "And remember, this needs to be on the outside around your waist. There is no on-off button, so you don't have to worry about powering it up when using it. The battery has a high-yield electromagnetic density that will give enough juice for a trip there and back. On the side panel is where we program the time, and the device stays on long enough to bring you to that particular moment along the space-time continuum."

"To the fourth dimension, the past *phase*, right?" Ford said.

"*Da*. And this button here brings you back to the present phase. You don't have to set it because the device can't bring you into the future, only to the current phase. I haven't figured that part out yet, but I'm working on it."

Alexander grabbed Sasha's shoulders. "Thanks, brother. We'll take it from here. Just bring us back to the future in one piece."

AFTER GATHERING THE ELECTROMAGNETIC TIME TRAVEL belts and the neural core sensory receptor, Alexander and Ford left Sasha and took another cab back to the magnarail station in Kiev, then back to Byzantium. The next deep submergence vehicle to Beirut didn't leave until the next morning, so the pair used the chance to rest up at a Ministerium monastery outside the city and grab a change of clothes for Ford to better fit in with AD 65. He had protested the tunic, questioning whether Alexander got the threads right, but he relented.

The next morning, they boarded the DSV using falsified credentials. Alexander was loath to engage more cloak-and-dagger routines, given what had happened the first time he'd donned Ministerium-issued contact lenses with Tara. This time, they sailed through without a hitch. An hour after shoving off from the coast, they docked at Beirut International Seaport.

The pair followed the crowd of travelers out into the late-afternoon city bustling with magnacars and pedestrians on magnaboards hovering across the street that flanked the seaport. A gentle breeze stole through the skyscrapers of gleaming titanium and glass shielding the world below from the punishing sun above. Wasn't worth much, since the dry, hot air still caused the men to instantly begin to perspire, but it was something.

Alexander hoisted the case holding the electromagnetic time belt around his shoulder and planted his hands on his hips. Glancing around the ultramodern city that mirrored much of the Republic circa AD 2123, he panicked wondering how in the world they would find a spot that coincided with Jude Thaddeus's phase of Beirut.

"Now what?" asked Ford, mirroring Alexander's posture and taking in the city.

"I was going to ask you the same question."

"Don't look at me. You're the expert in these matters. I'm just the hired muscle."

Alexander shook his head. "This isn't going to be easy. Patmos was basically left untouched from AD 95. But this..." He swept his hand across the cityscape.

"Why does it matter, anyhow? Can't we just pick a spot and tell it to beam us out of here to some other spot in the past?"

"Doesn't work like that. Sasha said the device only lets us... well, beam out, as you said, to the exact spot in another phase of time. Same for beaming back again. The device opens up a wormhole between both locations in space and time."

"Which means we don't want to end up popping out of the wormhole in some outhouse while some lady is taking care of business."

Alexander glanced at Ford with a raised brow. "Something like that."

The two started walking toward nowhere in particular, trying to figure out where to begin their journey.

"What about near the shoreline?" Ford offered. "Should be more desolate than the hustle and bustle of the city."

Alexander considered this. Wasn't a bad idea. "Alright. Let's check it out."

The shore was six blocks away beyond the seaport. But as they neared, Ford cursed.

"Not good, partner," Ford complained as they mounted the boardwalk that took them past a restaurant serving sushi and toward the shoreline. "Way too many buildings and peeps to get out of Dodge unannounced."

"That doesn't necessarily matter."

"Why not?"

"Because back then, in AD 65," Alexander explained, "this would have been pretty desolate. Probably just a wharf standing outside the city, but none of these restaurants and boardwalks. And even then, the change in climate has pushed the sea inland, so we could very well end up in a field."

"True that, I guess. So we jump from here?"

"Looks as good as any spot. Because like you said, we don't

want to pop out in somebody's house."

"Or a wall or tree for that matter."

Alexander looked at Ford and nodded, approaching a building that might just do the trick sitting off the boardwalk. It was a set of public restrooms maintained by the city. He walked up to the men's side and opened the door.

"Eww," Ford complained from the boardwalk. "You gotta take a leak that bad that you'd use a Republic pitstop?"

Alexander came out beaming. "All clear."

"Have at it then," he huffed, folding his arms.

"Not for using. For our time travel. We can lock the door and make the jump in private. It'll take a few hours, because apparently time travel takes some time. I would imagine people will think the restroom is out of order, but hopefully we won't jump back to the future while someone is, well, taking care of business as you said."

Ford tilted his head. "Hopefully not! Alright, let's roll, partner."

The man followed Alexander inside. Alexander took a parting glance, then shut and locked the door.

Ford was already taking out his belt; Alexander followed suit with his own, as well as the neural core sensory receptor.

"Let me help you with that, partner," Ford said, fastening the cap onto Alexander's head, pressing the top button when he was finished.

Five tentacles sprang from beneath to attach to his head. The familiar sensory distortion feeling washed over Alexander, unnerving him as before. His vision dimmed for a moment, his hearing following the same pattern as the cap connected to the synapses of his visual and aural brain neurons.

Alexander took a stabilizing breath and blinked his eyes. He turned his head from side to side and put out his arms, feeling like he was going to fall over.

"You OK, dude?" asked Ford. "You look worse than a drunken Solterra soldier."

"I'm fine." He squinted and shook his head, then turned it from side to side again. "Just some sort of delay in my vision and hearing. This happened last time. Like vertigo." He wobbled his head again and eased in and out another breath.

"Sounds trippy." Ford handed Alexander his belt, then retrieved his own.

Alexander fastened the time transport belt around his waist, then engaged the screen situated on the front while Ford did the same. A little screen on each of their devices displayed a Cyrillic word in green. The word *GO*, indicating all was ready to jump phases.

Alexander's heart leaped, anxiety beginning to course through his veins at the memory of what he had experienced the last time—and what they would experience again. He started breathing heavier as his pulse started picking up pace, realizing this was it, again. The moment of truth.

He prayed they jumped to the past phase of the early Church without incident, rather than ending up a scrambled mass of atoms and molecules on the restroom floor.

"So what's next, partner?" asked Ford.

"We need to set the time coordinates." Alexander took out his mobile device and rang Sasha. He picked up on the first buzz.

"About time you be calling me! How is everything being?"

"We made it, and we've attached the devices. We're ready to jump phases."

"*Otlichno!* So what phase will you be jumping to again?"

Alexander replied, "Father Jim said AD 65 would make the most sense, given where Jude Thaddeus was at and what he was doing at the time."

"AD 65 it is." Sasha commanded his terminal to set the coordinates two millennia in the past.

"Ooh-kee-doh-kee, Alex. I just set the coordinates for AD 65. That big green Ukrainski word should be flashing now."

Alexander looked down to see that the Cyrillic word for GO was flashing green. He nodded. "Looks like we're all set."

"Then you know what to do."

Indeed, he did. His heart started thrumming against his ribcage, his breath catching in his chest at what he knew would happen next.

Phase jumping. Time travel.

"Hold on for the second ride of your life, my friend," Sasha said before signing off.

Alexander's gut twisted with anticipation as he stowed his mobile device. His frayed nerves were beginning to hum with excitement now for what he was about to embark on. But then a peace began to descend upon him as his fingers flexed in readiness to jump with both feet again through the looking glass of Ichthus's past.

He took a stabilizing breath and looked at Ford. "You ready?"

The man sucked in a stabilizing breath of his own then nodded. "Let's do this."

Alexander nodded and showed Ford where to press the blinking GO button to make the jump back to phase AD 65.

Ford said he understood and that he was ready, flexing his fingers and hovering his left index finger over the device screen.

"Right then," Alexander said. "Next stop, Jude Thaddeus's house."

The two closed their eyes, heaved a collective breath, jammed their fingers onto the flashing screen, clenched their teeth, and waited for the journey that would take them back through time.

CHAPTER 16

ALL AT ONCE, Alexander's body began vibrating in long, undulating waves, the familiar sensation that was warm and fluid, like being dunked into a simmering jacuzzi just as a live wire was thrust inside.

The sensation was exactly as he remembered it from a week ago. It was positively delightful and all at once maddening!

As he zoomed through time, every one of his molecules tingled, set on edge by the electromagnetic force field. He felt every fiber of his being set on edge, as if walking across the carpet in wool socks and kicking up a static charge that reverberated all across his body. All five senses were on cloud nine, a high greater than the narcowafers nestled in his pocket.

There was the smell, as inviting and electrifying as the first time. It reminded him of the moment right after a midsummer Tripolitanian storm, when the Mediterranean air was charged by spiderwebbey streaks of lightning, sweet yet a peculiar mixture of salt and spice in his mouth. Oddly tasting like one of the wines he vinified from the berries he harvested along the bluff of his parish, with a heavy tannic acidity that set his taste buds on edge.

It was also bright, like a nuclear explosion had detonated around him. Again, the words of Oppenheimer popped back into his head: *'If the radiance of a thousand suns were to burst at once into the sky, that would be like the splendor of the mighty one.'* Except there wasn't any heat to it all. Just a steady temperature that seemed perfectly tuned to his body. He squeezed his eyes as he vibrated and tingled from the present to the past, fearing again that he would go blind from time's movement.

Then there was the sound of it all. Which was zero. Zip. Zilch. None whatsoever. It was like he was encased in a vacuum sealed off from reality, without any indication that a world, full of the bassy and trebley ranges of modern life, still existed on the outside. No hum, no tuning-fork ting. And there was a pressure within his inner head that he didn't recall before. He chanced swallowing and moving his jaw, trying to get his ears to pop, but it was no use.

He tried sensing John Mark Ford as he rode the waves of time alongside him, but it was as if he were all alone in a capsule of soundless, blinding, tingly, sweet-and-salty nirvana that smelled of electrified rain, stepping higher and higher to greater heights of sensory euphoria.

Then all at once, it stopped, as suddenly as it started. No more tingling, no more warm fluidity, no more static scent of thunderstorms, no more blinding luminescence and soundless pressure.

For a moment, he again thought he was dead, his atoms ending up in a rearranged pile of goop this time.

Then he heard all he needed to hear to let him know he had once again made it to the other side of the jump, both him and his partner still intact.

"Pee-yew!" Ford exclaimed, "What the crap is that smell —literally?"

Alexander threw open his eyes, then spun around and

scanned the area for anyone who would spot their entrance. Blessedly, there didn't seem to be a soul around.

And for good reason.

He made the mistake of heaving lungfuls of air after the jump, wincing and regretting his decision to not heed his partner's warning.

Boy, did it smell! Like a barnyard combined with a sewage treatment plant and compost pile of rotting vegetables and spoiled beef.

He moaned, realizing where they had landed.

The town garbage dump!

The sun was suspended high in a clear sky, punctuated by floating vultures and turkey buzzards, offering an unrelenting heat that boiled the dump into a steaming, humid, suffocating miasma of putrid rottenness. Alexander continued scanning the area, finding they were just outside Beirut on the south side of town.

His head started spinning from the unrelenting smell, his breaths thick and hot and triggering his gag reflex. He pivoted for a turn to catch sight of Ford when his foot slipped on something slimy, nearly sending him to the ground of rot.

"Eww," he complained, lifting a foot that had been standing on a mushy head of cabbage gone grayish green.

As he balanced on one leg, he threw his forearm against his face and tried filtering his breaths, but it was no use. Small mounds of trash—food and broken pottery and other miscellany from first-century Roman life—littered the area along with what was surely human or animal excrement.

"Eww is right," Ford agreed. "You couldn't have coordinated our jump through time to a better smelling LZ?" The man was holding his own leg up, something brown having stuck to the bottom of a sandal.

Alexander stifled a giggle, but it slipped through. Which

turned into a full-on belly laugh at the sight of what was surely crap stuck to the bottom of Ford's shoe combined with the image of him standing like a flamingo. The adrenaline high from having survived another jump through time fueled his continued laughter. He'd cheated death once again.

He had jumped phases of time once again!

"I swear, if you don't quit it, Zarruq, I'll fling this pile of poo your way without a second thought."

"Sorry," Alexander said, composing himself. Another snicker slipped through his nose before his face grew serious and he offered his hands in surrender. "Won't happen again."

Ford threw him a look, then glanced down at his still-suspended foot, scrunching up his face with irritated disgust and frantically looking for a place to land it.

"Let's get the heck out of here," he finally said. "I prefer that my garbage be promptly whisked away underground through Solterra-issued pneumatic tubes and recycled than an open-air, steaming pile of shi—"

"Alright, Johnny Mark," Alexander interrupted. "Got it. And I agree, but where?"

He scanned the area again and released the electromagnetic time belt from around his waist. He slung it over his shoulder and said, "And we've got to hide these things. Can't very well lug them through town now, can we?"

Ford followed his lead, unhooking his own time travel belt and slinging it around his neck like a python. Suddenly, he doubled over and let out a belch before a stream of yellowish puke poured out of his mouth.

Alexander almost snickered again, slightly pleased to see the macho man lose his lunch. But he thought against it. Could very well have been him. Might be him soon if they didn't get out of there pronto.

He put a hand on the man's shoulder. "Sorry, brother. Follow me. I think I found something that might work."

Ford wiped his mouth on his sleeve and nodded, his face sheet-white and lips still glistening with yellow bile.

"Hold up!" Ford said as Alexander took off.

He spun around. "What?"

"I'm no expert at this time travel gig like you, but shouldn't we, like, mark our spot? You know, so that we don't go zooming back to the future and end up getting our butts roasted by some kitchen burner, or worse?"

Good idea. Alexander searched the area for some sort of landmark. His eyes caught sight of a large faded red amphora pot, the kind that might hold water or flour. It was marked with use, bits having been chipped out around the lip of the pot. Other than that, it was a perfectly fine vessel.

And he thought the throwaway culture of ultramodernity was bad.

"This should do. It's big, it's red."

"And intact," Ford noted.

He lugged the pot over to where Ford was standing.

"Wait, you're gonna use that?" he said.

Alexander eyed it. "Yeah. Is there a problem?"

"Well, back in my dumpster-diving days—"

"Dumpster-diving days?" Alexander interrupted.

"Hey, don't judge! As I was going to say, this here's a fine specimen ripe for the taking. What if someone comes looking for a well-loved pot and nabs our only X-marks-the-spot?"

"You're just being paranoid," he scoffed, turning toward a mound he spotted to hide their belts.

Ford shook his head. "I'm just saying. Maybe we should find something else to—"

"Do you see anything else here besides fifty variations of pot shards and poo? Didn't think so. It's the only chance we've got to marking our spot, as you said. We're good. And if I'm wrong, I'll eat my hat."

Nearly stepping in another pile of poo himself, Alexander huffed off, counting his steps carefully and leading them toward a large boulder the size of a prize-winning hog sitting several yards away in the middle of the field of refuse.

Ford shook his head but relented and followed his lead, covering his nose and mouth with one arm and clenching his stomach with the other.

They reached the oversized rock, soaked from the high-noon sun and from being overcome by the putrid smell. There was an opening on one side that ran underneath the fat mound. Some sort of animal den, perhaps a fox or a badger.

Alexander bent to his knees and eyed the hole. Satisfied, he took a breath and stuck his arm inside. All clear.

He slung his belt off from his shoulder. "It'll be tight, but they should both fit. The boulder will offer good coverage and an easy landmark for later. And I doubt anyone will venture out this far, given all the garbage—"

"And crap!" Ford growled.

Alexander smiled and nodded. "And, yes, the crap. Give me your belt."

Ford handed him his device and Alexander stuffed them both inside.

He grabbed a few shards of reddish pottery thrown a yard away and leaned them against the opening. Standing, he lined up his arm with an imperial statue that lay beyond their marked jump point at the edge of the beige and brown town. Then he recounted his paces back to Ford and their jump point, a fail-safe to ensure they didn't end up somewhere unfortunate.

"Alright. *Now*, let's get the heck out of here."

THE PAIR MADE QUICK WORK DARTING THROUGH THE garbage dump, making for a cluster of beige buildings made of brick, roofed by logs and straw. They came up alongside an outer wall, slowed and composed themselves, scraping the refuse and other remains off from their sandals against the rocky ground.

"Shall we?" Alexander said, taking a breath and girding himself for the mission beyond the garbage dump.

"Locked and loaded, partner."

Alexander startled. "You brought your sidearm with you?" he exclaimed.

Ford scoffed. "Of course not, dingleberry. It was a figure of speech." He clenched a hand on Alexander's shoulder then continued onward. "Come on. It's go time."

He huffed and followed after the man, rounding the corner into the main town.

And nearly colliding with a short, stout woman bearing a large clay jug on her head.

She gasped, eyes going wide at the surprise and throwing her hands on the side of the jar to stabilize it. She slung a string of words in Aramaic at them, the tongue of the region.

Alexander turned to make an attempt at reconciliation, digging deep into the well of his graduate school training in the original tongue of Jesus' day. But Ford grabbed his tunic and dragged him forward.

"Leave it and let's keep moving. No need to draw any more attention to us than we already are coming out of the garbage dump."

Alexander nodded and continued, taking lead. The pair made their way through a narrow street edged by what looked like homes and small shops of the same dull beige bricks, roofs blotting out the sunshine, yet almost as suffocating as the trash heap. And just as smelly, a mixture of boiling vegetables and rot.

They kept walking in silence through the darkened street, trying their best to avoid bumping into anyone else. The narrow streets were crammed with people going this way and that—mothers wearing plain white sacks for dresses and their children wearing long white shirts; men with pants and tunics like the time travelers were wearing, proving that Alexander was right, despite Ford's protests.

A soft crunch sounded behind Alexander. He glanced back and startled with irritation.

"Where the heck did you get that?" he hissed, pulling Ford aside and pointing at a bright red apple he was removing from his mouth after his bite.

Mid-chew, the man suspended his mouth open with confusion. "From the cafeteria back at the Ministerium."

"You've been carrying around an apple all this time and didn't let me know?"

"Uh, yeah," he said, continuing to chew his bite.

"And you brought it on our trip through time?"

"Uh, yeah...Why, you want a bite?"

"No, I don't want a bite! How do we know they had apples back in the day, in AD 65 in Beirut?"

Ford swallowed and held his apple up to his face, eyeing it. "Well, Mama Eve ate one back in the day in Mesopotamia, which isn't so far from here. Figured it'd be alright."

"Good Lord..." Alexander scoffed, then mumbled something about the state of Christian education. "It wasn't an apple, moron. Look, it doesn't matter. Sasha said we can't change history with our little movements, like introducing a non-indigenous piece of fruit several centuries before its time. Finish the blasted thing, core and all, and let's get going."

He turned to leave, but grabbed the apple and took a bite,

handing it back to Ford and chewing some before swallowing it whole. "There. Now we can get going. And I would appreciate you not holding out on me next time."

Ford saluted Alexander and followed after him. "Yes, sir. Sorry 'bout that. Didn't much take you for the apple-eating type."

Alexander rolled his eyes and went to say something when they rounded another corner and the street opening up. It was lined with wooden carts sporting brightly colored canopies selling pottery and slabs of beef, sickly looking vegetables and dried herbs. It looked like some sort of town marketplace.

A wind gusted past them bearing the heavenly scent of saffron and roasted meat, followed by the scent of the sea—salt and fish and rotting seaweed. The street was loud, with vendors shouting for potential patrons to sample their wares and customers haggling for better prices. Someone else banged on a tambourine and another tooted away on some instrument while another offered a mercilessly off-key rendition of some Syrian ballad.

"Good Lord, do you smell," Alexander complained as they walked through the gauntlet of vendors.

Ford slugged him in the arm. "Speak for yourself, partner. And I don't think it's me or you. Well, only me or you. I think the past just reeks to high heaven!"

A ways through the market maze, the cramped street opened further into a square of buildings with even more market stalls, commanded by a large fountain in the center. Women were collecting its precious water in jugs and children were splashing inside for relief.

"Heaven..." Ford said, darting for the water without consulting Alexander.

But he agreed. The heat was merciless, and perhaps the water could wash away some of their stink.

Ford hustled up next to a woman who had just hefted a reddish jar pockmarked with use off her head, and he palmed two helpings of water onto his face. Alexander did the same when he caught up.

The man wasn't too far off the mark. The cool freshness of the spring water brought into the town by lead piping from nearby aqueducts was indeed heaven.

The woman glanced at them, then leaned over and dunked her jar into the water.

Ford looked at her, then to her jar and shrugged. He leaned over the flagstone ledge himself and dunked his head into the water. The woman squealed and other women a few down gasped at the sight.

Alexander apologized for his friend as the man brought his head out. "No need to draw any attention to us, eh?"

"It's hot as Hades out here," Ford said, the water still dribbling down his face. He wiped it back over his head, then added, "But my oh my, was that refreshing. You should try it."

"I think I'll pass."

"Suit yourself. Your loss." Ford glanced around to either side of them as the women scurried away. He folded his arms and leaned against the ledge. "Now what?"

Alexander did the same. "Now we pray the good Lord sends us a miraculous sign."

A voice rose above the din of the rushing fountain water and clamoring sounds of the marketplace.

The word *Yeshua Msheekha* rose even higher.

He immediately understood the Aramaic.

Jesus the Messiah.

Alexander pushed off from the fountain and spun around, searching for the open-air evangelist declaring the name of his Savior and Lord.

Over there. A man standing on the stairs of a large building commanding the north side of the plaza, shouting what Alexander discerned were lines from the Gospels.

"Where's the four-alarm fire, partner?" asked Ford.

"Come on," Alexander said, rushing over to the evangelist.

"Why, what's there?" Ford shouted after him.

"Our miracle!"

CHAPTER 17

"As Jesus started on his way," the evangelist boomed from the stairs in Aramaic, "a man ran up to him and fell on his knees before him. *'Good teacher,'* he asked, *'what must I do to inherit eternal life?'*"

Alexander and Ford hustled over to the crowd of onlookers as the man started teaching a familiar passage. From what the Church would later call the Gospel of Mark, a biographical sketch of the life of Jesus included in the Holy Scriptures.

The man continued his sermon: "*'Why do you call me good?' Jesus answered. 'No one is good—except God alone. You know the commandments: You shall not murder, you shall not commit adultery, you shall not steal, you shall not give false testimony, you shall not defraud, honor your father and mother.'*"

"*'Teacher,'* the man declared, *'all these I have kept since I was a boy.'*"

"Hey I recognize this," Ford whispered. "Ain't it something about the rich entering into heaven? From Mark's Gospel?"

"*'Jesus looked at him and loved him,'*" the evangelist continued. "*'One thing you lack,' he said. 'Go, sell everything you have and give to the poor, and you will have treasure in heaven. Then come, follow me.'*"

Alexander nodded. "You're right. But not about heaven. The kingdom of God."

Ford went to respond when the evangelist boomed again, coming to the climax of the teaching: "At this the man's face fell. He went away sad, because he had great wealth.

"Jesus looked around and said to his disciples, *'How hard it is for the rich to enter the kingdom of God!'*"

A murmur raced through the crowd of onlookers. But no one walked away. In fact, more gathered around the group, coming up behind and leaning in to listen.

"Can you imagine such a thing?" the evangelist asked, his voice bassy and sturdy. "In Jesus' day, the rich would certainly have been expected to be given entrance into God's kingdom. For their wealth was considered a sure sign of God's favor. And yet, *Yeshua Msheekha* said differently."

Another tremor of confusion and curiosity wound its way through the crowd. The hairs on Alexander's arms and neck stood on end from the experience. There he was, standing in the soil Jesus himself could very well have walked, listening to someone familiar with the memory of his teachings. Perhaps even one of his disciples.

But who was this guy?

He continued, reciting from what became the Gospel of Mark: "The disciples were amazed at his words. But Jesus said again, *'Children, how hard it is to enter the kingdom of God! It is easier for a camel to go through the eye of a needle than for someone who is rich to enter the kingdom of God.'*

"The disciples were even more amazed, and said to each other, *'Who then can be saved?'*"

The man paused, his face growing serious. Then he said, "Jesus looked at them and said, *'With man this is impossible, but not with God; all things are possible with God.'*

"Then Peter spoke up, *'We have left everything to follow you!'*"

He paused again, a smile playing across his face. He chuckled and shook his head, closing his eyes as if reliving a memory. Then he said, "*'Truly I tell you,'* Jesus replied, *'no one who has left home or brothers or sisters or mother or father or children or fields for me and the gospel will fail to receive a hundred times as much in this present age: homes, brothers, sisters, mothers, children and fields—along with persecutions—and in the age to come eternal life. But many who are first will be last, and the last first.'*"

"I urge you, therefore," the man said, "to count the cost and follow the one who was sacrificed for the sins of the world, the King of Kings and Lord of Lords!"

"Caesar is Lord!" one man shouted not far from Alexander. Another affirmed him, raising a fist and repeating the mantra he had heard about, but only from the distance of New Testament history.

Something sailed from over Alexander's shoulder and struck the side of the building just above the evangelist. A vegetable of some sort, rotten and smearing wet down its face.

The man dodged out of the way as another few pieces sailed toward him. One hitting high, two striking him in the head and arm. He stumbled down the stairs to the dusty ground, a wooden cane following close behind with a clatter.

The crowd began dispersing, clearly not wanting to be around if the Roman authorities came calling.

Alexander strode up a meter from the man, wearing a dirty beige tunic with ruddy brown skin and crooked nose, hair long and curly and unkempt falling down to his shoulders. He offered the man his arm, helping him right himself up again.

The evangelist startled but offered a smile and a nod. He

reached for Alexander's arm with one hand and his wooden cane with the other, then said in Aramaic, "Thank you, kind sir."

"Certainly," Alexander replied in the same tongue.

The man stood and brushed his tunic, then touched his head where he had been hit. He wasn't bleeding, but Alexander was sure it would leave a mark. He took in a breath and scanned the area, then closed his eyes and mumbled something that sounded like a prayer. *Amen,* he said when he was finished.

"My name is Simon, dear fellow," he said, stretching out his hand. "And yours?"

Alexander hesitated, glancing at Ford but deciding there wouldn't be any harm in revealing their names. "Alexander," he replied, taking the man's gesture. "I appreciated your words."

The corners of his mouth tugged into a hopeful grin. "Really?" Simon penetrated Alexander with deep chocolate eyes, as if searching for something.

There was a tap on the ground with Simon's cane.

Alexander looked down. In the dust was a line, arching and unfinished.

He furrowed his brow, taking a beat to discern its meaning.

Then it hit him.

The signal.

His heart quickened and breath grew labored with the excitement of what he was being asked to do.

Complete the arc.

He slowly knelt to the ground, then he drew the corresponding arc on the mirror side that intersected near the end.

Forming the *ichthus* that signaled the two were friends, brothers in *Yeshua Msheekha.*

Alexander stood and Simon immediately grabbed him in a

bear hug, planting a kiss of greeting on both cheeks. "What a joy to meet fellow brothers in the Lord Jesus Christ!"

"You people back in the day weren't kidding about greeting one another with a holy kiss, were you?" Ford complained in the same Aramaic, his face twisted with a look of disgust.

Alexander threw him a look, but he was also impressed with the man's language skills.

Simon asked, "And who might you be?"

"This here is John Mark," Alexander offered, responding before Ford could say anything stupid again.

Simon raised a brow. "I know a good man named John Mark. A friend who documented the very things I spoke about earlier. In fact," he said, turning to Alexander. "A man who looks very much like you."

Alexander's breath seized in his chest; his eyes went wide with possibility.

Could it really be him?

He knew that the unbroken tradition of the Church was that John Mark was the same man who wrote the Gospel of Mark. Who documented the very things that Simon was speaking about. Tradition also puts his origins of birth at Cyrene of Cyrenaica, on the eastern edge of what was now Tripolitania back in Solterra, the future.

His homeland.

Alexander's mind was racing with potential. Because there was a possibility this man knew the apostle Mark. Which meant he was a disciple of Jesus!

Simon...

Probably wasn't Simon Peter, the apostle and so-called "rock" upon which Christ said he would build the Church. His evangelistic work took him to Rome. And besides, he had probably been martyred by now.

But there was another Simon.

Simon the Zealot.

Who also traveled with Jude Thaddeus.

Alexander cleared his throat. Now or never.

"If you don't mind my saying," he said, "you don't look like you would be from around here."

The man chuckled. "No, I am not from Syria. However, I was born not far away."

"And where was that?" Ford asked, taking the hint that something important lay beneath the surface.

"Cana, of Samaria."

Bingo.

Both Matthew and John Mark identified Simon the Zealot as Simon the Canaanite.

"Tell me, brother Simon," Alexander said, doing everything within his power to hide his glee. "What of brother Thaddeus? Do you have news of his whereabouts?"

"Do I have news?" asked Simon, raising a brow.

I overreached...

In his eagerness to tie the two together and find their target's location, he spooked the man. Probably thought they were sent by Emperor Nero himself to hunt down the People of the Way, round them up and send them to the Colosseum for his lion mauling and fire-burning spectacles!

The man replied, "I have something better than news. I have the man himself!"

"Well, I'll be," Ford said.

Simon looked at him, confused.

"The reason I asked, brother Simon," Alexander said, trying to recover, "is that I heard his letter read, err, a while ago...and it served to exhort me to contend for the faith that was once for all entrusted to me. To God's holy people, as he wrote." He paused to catch his breath. He swallowed, then continued, "And, well, I would very much like to meet the apostle, to thank him for his encouraging words."

Simon laid a hand upon his shoulder and smiled. "Right this way, brother Alexander. I will take you to him. You and John Mark here."

Alexander flashed Ford a victorious grin.

Now they were getting somewhere.

CHAPTER 18

Simon led Alexander and Ford through the market crowded with carts and even more customers bartering for the wares of the merchants.

The sun seemed to hang with mocking intent in the clear afternoon sky, boiling the world down below with merciless, suffocating heat. It didn't help matters they were wading through a sea of overripe bodies in desperate need of a good dousing.

Movement through the market square was slow going, and Simon kept glancing back toward his new companions to make sure he hadn't lost them. He hadn't. But the cacophony of the square and pressing bodies, compounded by the suffocating heat, made it difficult to follow.

A man rammed into Alexander's right side, sending him face-first into the back of Ford's head. He bit his lip in the exchange, and his mouth instantly filled with the taste of tangy copper.

"Ouch!" Ford shouted, lunging forward and rubbing the back of his head as that corner of the market erupted in shouts of protest between the man and a merchant and several more onlookers.

"Sorry!" Alexander said back, wincing as he licked his lips to check the damage. From what little he could understand in the shouting, the man who ran into him was accused of stealing something from the merchant.

"You alright, partner?" asked Ford.

"I'm fine. Let's keep going. I don't want us to get caught up in this mess if the praetorian guard arrives."

"Roger that." He turned to leave, but stopped short. "Do you see our new friend?"

Alexander scanned the swarm of bodies, the people and tones all running together.

Panic started setting in quick. He was their only lifeline to the object of their mission, Jude Thaddeus. And they let him get away.

No, I let him get away through clumsy carelessness!

He pushed through and hustled forward, then stood on his toes for a better look.

No sign of him.

His mouth started watering for the narcowafers, and his breath ran quick and hot in his mouth and nose at the rising panic, the cacophony of the market not helping matters.

Where the heck did he—

There was a high-pitched whistle, and then he heard his name above the marketplace din.

Alexander spun around until he found Ford raising up Simon's arm and motioning for him to follow.

He closed his eyes and sighed with relief then caught up to the pair. "I thought I had lost you."

"Almost had," Ford said.

"Let's get out of here."

Simon darted through the crowds, and the two pushed forward after him.

Until another man stepped in his way, hunchbacked with

greasy, graying wavy hair down to his shoulders and smelling as ripe as the garbage dump.

He was holding a rope weighed down with stiff dead rodents. He slung rapid Aramaic at Alexander offering them "For good price and tasty meal!"

Ford brushed past Alexander and continued following Simon as he thanked the man kindly, trying to peel himself away and continue on. But to no avail.

The man grabbed his wrist and shoved the rope at him, his eyes pleading and desperate.

Alexander yanked it back.

I'm not cut out for the past, he silently complained to himself, then ran after his companion.

Several more blocks later, Simon darted down an alleyway that ran the length of a three-story building with warped walls that looked like it could topple inside the corridor at any minute.

At the end, a modest one-level dwelling of the same beige bricks with a sturdy wooden door stood proud amidst the decaying rubble.

Simon hustled toward it, looking over his shoulders. He stopped short and knocked three times, then twice more as his two companions reached his side.

A few seconds later, there was an unlatching of locks. The man pushed through the door, ushering them inside.

"Brother Jude," Simon said. "We have ourselves some visitors."

"Visitors you say," replied a man sounding raspy with age.

"Plucked them up from the market, I did!" he said, holding the door open for the two.

Alexander went first, nearly taking his shawl off when he remembered the neural immersive device resting underneath. Ford followed, then closed the door.

"Alexander and John Mark," Simon introduced them. "Fellow brothers in the Lord Jesus."

"John Mark, you say?" Jude Thaddeus said, eyeing the two men suspiciously.

"Uh, yes, John Mark Fo—err...I mean," he stumbled. Giving his surname would have been a major miss, given the ancients didn't have such names like the future. "Yes, John Mark," Ford said before taking a step back and smiling, motioning toward Alexander.

Alexander took a step forward and extended his hand in greeting. When he did, the man looked at it with furrowed brow.

The time travel stuff was tough to navigate, with knowing ancient customs and all. So he opted to try and smooth over his mistake by opening up into an embrace. Jude nodded and obliged.

"Pleasure making your acquaintance, you two. And fellow believers in Jesus Christ you say?"

Alexander nodded. "That's right."

"And where were you baptized?"

"Uh..." he faltered, glancing at Ford.

Who picked up the ball, saying, "The River Jordan."

Jude's eyes widened at the name, the river probably carrying special significance for the man, as well as all Christians during that era, given Jesus had been baptized in it. "Splendid! And where are you both from then?"

"Tripolitania, sir," Ford offered.

Alexander sucked in a worried breath, but remembered that his future home region was named after the ancient Roman one.

"Dear me!" exclaimed Simon this time. "You've traveled far from home, haven't you?"

He offered an even more worried sigh. Great.

"Yes, well..." Alexander stammered, "we came to Judea seeking adventure."

"Don't we all at that age!" Jude said. "Did you find any?"

Alexander chuckled. "You could say that."

"Good, good." The man made a startled leaping motion and waved them further inside the modest dwelling. "Make yourselves at home. I was just preparing for the agape feast later this evening. However, perhaps we shall partake earlier."

Alexander grabbed Ford's arm, grinning with wide eyes at the possibility of celebrating the Eucharist with an original disciple of Christ—partaking of the body-and-blood memory-markers that he himself witnessed firsthand through Jesus' crucifixion and the Last Supper before that.

The men gathered around a squat table made of hearty wood with red and blue woven cushions surrounding it. Jude Thaddeus motioned for them to sit and recline around the communal piece of furniture.

Blessedly, and surprisingly, the room wasn't as stifling as the outside. A gentle breeze blew easily through large vacant windows, tattered curtains waving in quiet response and the smell of a salty sea filling the place, along with what smelled of freshly baked bread. Alexander's mouth began to water at the smells dueling for his attention. The home looked to be sitting on the outskirts of town overlooking the Mediterranean a few hundred meters away. The sun illuminated the place, as well as a few well-placed candles to fill in the gaps.

Simon carried a loaf of bread wrapped in cheesecloth over from a stone oven and set it in the middle of the table. Jude Thaddeus bore a clay jar of wine and a wooden cup, setting both in the middle of the table to join what would be the host. The Body of Christ.

"Alexander, here, tells me he caught wind of your letter," Simon said as they settled down for the afternoon.

"Oh?" Jude said, perking up with interest.

Alexander nodded. "Yes, sir. Thank you, sir. I...err, heard of some of its content awhile back. The bit about contending for the once-for-all faith entrusted to the Church struck a chord. Wanted the opportunity to thank you for the words and ask about its origin. What made you want to write it?"

Jude Thaddeus smiled and settled back against a large pillow resting against a beige wall. "Yes, well, as you know, I wrote it to circulate amongst the churches throughout Asia and Galatia and Cappadocia to address specific situations plaguing Christ's body. But I truly wrote it to all the beloved who have been called by God the Father and kept safe in Jesus Christ."

"As well you should have," Alexander offered. "It is a message for all to hear." He paused, then added: "Both now and later, for future generations."

"Yes, well," the apostle went on, "I was eagerly preparing to write to them about our shared salvation. But instead I found it necessary, compelled really, to write and urge the Church to struggle and contend for the once-for-all faith delivered, committed, entrusted to the saints. For certain people had secretly slipped in amongst them, whose condemnation was long ago written about."

"Who?" Ford asked.

Jude Thaddeus smirked and shook his head bitterly. "Ungodly, vile people who pervert the grace of our God into a license to engage in outrageous, debauched behavior and deny our only Sovereign and Lord, Jesus Christ. I thought it important to remind believers that the Lord at one time delivered his people out of the land of Egypt, but later destroyed those who did not believe."

"Believe..." Alexander mumbled, trailing off in slight conviction after his own struggles of late.

The man widened his eyes and took a breath. Nodding, he

said, "Yes, believe. Believing has always acted as the binding agent between God and his people, even from our ancestors, the people of Israel. And not only them, but the angels themselves who did not keep their own position of authority but left behind their proper dwelling—until the great judgment day, the Lord has kept them in eternal chains under the darkest of darkness. Likewise, Sodom and Gomorrah and all of the surrounding cities, which in exactly the same manner as they, lived immorally, indulging in sexual sin and pursuing unnatural fleshly desire—they serve as an example of suffering a punishment of eternal fire."

Punishment of eternal fire...

Alexander grimaced at the notion. That God could—that he *would*—punish with eternal fire. People and angels alike. But the man was clearly convinced and convicted of the need to emphasize the truth of it, given he was rehearsing the very words of his letter before them now.

"Woe to them, as I wrote!" Jude continued. "They have taken the way of Cain; they have rushed for profit into Balaam's error; they have been destroyed in Korah's rebellion."

The man closed his eyes and made a sputtering sound in disgust, shaking his head again at the rehearsal of his words that he had originally written down in his letter.

"They are clouds without rain, blown along by the wind; autumn trees, without fruit and uprooted—twice dead. They are wild waves of the sea, foaming up their shame; wandering stars, for whom the blackest darkness has been reserved forever."

"In what way?" asked Alexander.

Jude Thaddeus adjusted his posture and huffed, as if disgusted with even making mention of the false teachers. "Itinerate preachers, they are, infiltrating the churches with a message that takes the Corinthian slogan 'All things are lawful for me' to new extremes! These vile creatures have a peculiar blend of false teaching and false living, marrying theological doctrine that denies the one and only faith with rebellious practices that assault the very name of God. Which of course goes hand in hand."

"How so?" asked Ford.

"And you're saying these people disbelieve in God?" Alexander added.

Jude Thaddeus shifted and replied, "It isn't that they disbelieve God, but that they are morally rebelling against him. Leveraging the grace of God to engage in all sorts of morally repugnant behavior. Chief among them the kind of sexual immorality that Empire Rome not only tolerates, but celebrates and honors. And we all know what I mean by that!"

Alexander nodded, understanding that the kind of sexual immorality included in Jewish and Christian vice lists were a sharp contrast to the wicked practices of the surrounding culture. Not only drunken orgies that often centered on imperial sex cults, and the perverse practices of animal sexual penetration—men and women alike. But your run-of-the-mill fornication and adultery from the general population, as well as men penetrating men, and women exchanging natural relations with men for women.

"Cheap grace is all these evildoers peddle," the apostle continued. "Completely ignoring the fundamental reality of the faith, that upon repentance and receipt of forgiveness, one is wholly committed to God in Christ. They claim God's love grants one license to sin more than before. Their behavior denies that Jesus is indeed their only Sovereign Lord, bending the knee instead to the Empire and the phallic monstrosities of Bacchus. Rejecting the moral demands of Christ, they are in fact disowning him as their Master and shaking their fist at his authority."

He took a drink of water and a breath, shaking his head and muttering something to himself.

The apostle continued, "That is why I quoted from the ancient book of Enoch from our ancestors' Scriptures, the seventh from Adam who prophesied about them: *'Behold! The Lord is coming with thousands of his holy ones to execute judgment against everyone, to convict everyone's soul concerning the ungodly deeds they have committed in such ungodly ways, and concerning the defiant words that ungodly sinners have spoken against him.'* It's all incredibly relevant to the Body of Christ's current lot, I dare say! These people are grumblers and fault-finders; they are pursuing their own lustful desires. And these loud-mouths speak with boastfulness, showing favoritism and flattery for the sake of gain."

Ford and Alexander nodded along. Even Simon was listening with interest, and he had to have heard the man's exhortations rehearsed countless times as his missionary companion.

"But, dear friends, as I wrote in my letter," Jude Thaddeus continued, "remember the predictions foretold by the apostles of our Lord Jesus Christ. For they said to you, *'In the end times there will be mockers, scoffers who will pursue their own ungodly, lustful desires.'* These are those people who cause divisions, unspiritual ones, who do not have the Spirit. And this is one of the greatest dangers of the last times in which we are living. In which any generation of the Church will live."

Alexander nodded, thinking about the same sorts of divisions roiling the Church in his day back in the future.

"Ahh, but you, dear friends," the man continued, pointing at Alexander and Ford, "building yourselves up in your most holy faith and praying in the Holy Spirit, keep yourselves in the love of God, waiting for the mercy of our Lord Jesus Christ leading to eternal life."

Alexander smiled, captivated by the man. He glanced over at Ford, who himself was grinning with entranced concentration.

"Remember, Alexander and John Mark, on the one hand be merciful to those who are doubting, and on the other save others by snatching them out of the fire, and to others still show mercy with fear—hating even the garments defiled and stained by the sinful flesh."

The two nodded along as the man continued his exhortation.

Then he closed his eyes and breathed deeply, resting his palms on the wooden table and lifting them upward. He eased his breath out of his nose, as if conjuring the Spirit of the Lord himself, and said, "Now to him who is able to keep you free from stumbling and present you before his glorious presence spotless, blameless, and with exceeding joy—to the only God our Savior through Jesus Christ our Lord be glory, majesty, power and authority, before all time, now and forevermore! Amen."

"*Amen!*" the three men said with hearty agreement.

Jude Thaddeus nodded, then smiled. "Forgive me for my impromptu exhortation. But sometimes I get carried away."

"Not at all," Alexander said. Then he leaned into the moment, trying to take advantage of the opportunity and their mission, remembering why they had travelled there in the first place. "I appreciate the words. I have to imagine you've seen it all. What with your missionary travels and all."

The man chuckled. "Indeed, I have!"

"And what stands out to you," Ford asked, "from your efforts spreadin' the gospel?"

Jude Thaddeus took in a deep, contemplative breath and stared out past the gently swaying curtain through the open-air window. The man wasn't very old, by most standards. Probably would have been a teenager during his days with Jesus, maybe an early young adult. Which put him somewhere in his fifties. But he looked a decade or two older, the weight of his experiences etched across his face.

A smile played on that face, then he answered, "That would be Edessa."

Simon hummed with agreement. "I would agree. Holds a special place in my heart as well."

The two men perked at the mention of the place, sitting up straighter and moving closer to the table for a better angle at diving into the piece of revelation.

"Edessa?" Ford asked, throwing a hopeful glance at Alexander. "What is that?"

"And why is that?" Alexander said. Something about the word struck a chord, a hint at a memory of something he had studied.

"Why, because of what happened when I visited the town of northern Syria. And also because of what I brought with me."

Alexander's heart began to gallop forward. He sensed a clue hidden deep within the recesses of the man's story.

"If you don't mind sharing, partner," Ford said, "we'd love to hear about it."

The apostle looked to Simon, who nodded his approval.

"Well then," Jude Thaddeus began, "before the crucifixion of our Lord, he received a letter."

"Excuse me," Ford interrupted. "A letter?"

"That's right."

"Like, from a pen pal?"

Alexander smacked Ford's leg and threw him a look for him to shut it. Jude Thaddeus cocked his head and simply stared at the man with furrowed brow.

"Forgive my friend, here," he said. "He gets confused sometimes. As you were saying, Jesus received a note of correspondence."

Jude Thaddeus nodded. "Indeed. From King Abgar."

The name had a familiar ring. It seemed connected to a memory Alexander held from graduate school. A scrap of a story from the early Church historian Eusebius, offering an account about the ancient King of Edessa who had sent a letter to Jesus inviting him to visit. But he couldn't quite make out the details. He was eager to hear more of Jude's story. And discover what clues it might hold for back in the future world.

"And what did King Abgar want?" he asked.

"He requested a visit of the prophet he had heard so much about from travelers returning to the region from Jerusalem," Jude Thaddeus answered, "desiring to make Jesus' acquaintance and hear his teachings. However, there was a more personal motivation to the invitation. He was suffering greatly from an incurable disease. Story upon story of the many mighty miracles that our Lord performed south of his kingdom in Judea and Galilee had reached the king's ears. And he himself wanted to taste the fruits of our Lord's miraculous bounty."

Ford leaned forward, eyes wide with interest. "So what happened? Did he go and meet with the king?"

"Unfortunately, Jesus had to decline. However, he promised the king that he would send along one of his disciples to cure him after his mission on earth was complete."

"After his death, you mean?"

"Exactly."

Alexander said, "And that disciple was you, wasn't it, brother Jude?"

He smiled and nodded. "Indeed. The disciples sent me along to heal the king..." The man trailed off, then stared out the window.

Ford glanced at Alexander, who shrugged. Seemed like he was holding something back, wondering if he should say more.

"At any rate, I met with the man and later established a church in the city. And that was that."

The apostle leaned back and stared back out the window, a smile flashing across his face and eyes narrowing slightly before he sighed and returned to the party.

Was there more that the man wasn't sharing?

"Now, Jude," Simon interrupted. "You know that healing wasn't the only thing the good King Abgar received."

Jude Thaddeus waved a dismissive hand.

"Go on, tell them why the city means so much to you. To me, to all the apostles of our Lord. And what it was you started there."

CHAPTER 19

"Simon is right," Jude Thaddeus said. "As I mentioned, the disciples sent me as an answer to King Abgar's request. By the power of the Holy Spirit, I was able to offer healing to many while in Edessa, including the king himself."

He paused, hesitating to continue. He took a breath, then said, "I also brought along with me something extraordinary: a linen cloth with a stunning likeness portrayed on its surface."

The apostle went quiet; the room fell silent. It was as if he was waiting for one of them to respond.

Ford took the bait.

He sucked in a surprised breath, as if the mystery suddenly revealed itself to him. Ford whispered, "On which one can see not only a face but an entire body..."

Then his eyes went wide. "The Holy Shroud..."

It took a beat, but Jude Thaddeus snapped his head at the man and scowled. "Holy Shroud?"

He stood and pounded the table, the cup of wine jostling and bread bouncing with the force of it all. Simon sprang to stabilize the vessel holding the memory-marker of Christ's shed blood, succeeding and righting it.

Jude Thaddeus shouted, "What know you of this cloth bearing the image of our Lord?"

Ford's eyes went wide; his tongue tripped over on itself. "N...nothing. Nothing at all, don't worry about it."

"Liar!" The apostle pounded the table again, rising to his knees. He shoved forward against the table and raised a fist prepared for action.

Causing Ford to scramble backwards, the cushions getting in the way of his retreat. "I've heard only rumors of such a holy relic," the man stammered, throwing his arms up in surrender.

Alexander's mind was racing from the possibility of it all. He recalled a lecture Father Jim had delivered during a seminar on the Gospels. Laid out all the historical evidence that not only proved Jesus' existence and ministry in the Roman province of Judea (Apparently, there were some who drummed up conspiracies that the man hadn't even existed). But also his crucifixion and, more importantly, his resurrection.

And one of the prime exhibits was the so-called Shroud of Turin, an image of a man seemingly imprinted on a burial linen many had puzzled over for centuries. He still recalled a picture of the image that showcased Jesus in repose: It bore the distinct impression of the man's closed eyes, a mustache and beard and long hair falling beyond his shoulders to the center of his back; his arms were crossed, one hand over the other, and engraved with several markings that looked like cuts or marks made by a beating; hundreds more of the same etchings shone brightly on the man's back and chest, crisscrossing each other at jagged right angles with more of the lacerations marring both of his legs; more marked the crown of his head and seemed to be dripping down his forehead.

Father Jim had said the story that the image told was clear: The man had suffered the worst kind of death imaginable. In the late twentieth century, a cross-section of leading experts—from criminologists to doctors, historians to physicists—all came to the conclusion that not only was it an image of a man who had been crucified, it had been done to the exact specifications according to the Gospel witness. And then just over a century ago—well, a century from back to the future—a Princeton professor not only proved the image was of Jesus Christ, but that it proved he arose from the dead.

And here he was, the man who had brought the Holy Shroud with him to Edessa in order to preserve it. To preserve the memory it bore: the memory of Christ's resurrection contained within it.

A rash of goose pimples tingled across his skin at the thought. And he felt like they were almost there, that something was about to be revealed.

"And so, receiving the likeness from the apostle," Ford muttered, "immediately he felt his leprosy was cleansed and gone. Having been instructed then by the apostle more clearly of the doctrine of truth, he asked about the likeness portrayed on the linen cloth. For when he had carefully inspected it, he saw that it did not consist of earthy colors, and he was astounded by its power."

"What's that you say, dear fellow?" asked Jude Thaddeus.

He shook his head and smiled. "Just a report I had heard of some strange goings on in Edessa because of that there image you brought."

"Strange? I dare not say strange. Miraculous, more like it!"

"Yes, of course."

Oh, Johnny Mark...

Alexander said, "Tell us more about this...image you bore. The Shroud of Christ."

The apostle cleared his throat. "After Jesus was raised from the dead to new life by the Father, he presented himself to us and continued ministering. Remarkably, there were still brothers who doubted. Even though they saw him with their very own eyes, they struggled to believe."

"Like Thomas?" Ford said. Alexander cleared his throat. "Or so rumor has it."

Jude Thaddeus smiled. "Yes, well, he wasn't the only one..."

That revelation was striking to Alexander. And the way the man spoke it seemed to indicate he himself had struggled to believe Jesus had been raised from the dead.

"And yet," the man continued, "Jesus never gave up on us. In fact, he continually presented himself to us and offered us further proof that what had unfolded over those few days—his brutal death at the hands of those bloodthirsty Romans, and his resurrection from the dead that third day—he proved it had indeed taken place."

Alexander was struck by his revelation, recalling something that had always puzzled him from the first chapter in the book of Acts: '*After his suffering, he presented himself to them and gave many convincing proofs that he was alive. He appeared to them over a period of forty days and spoke about the kingdom of God.*'

Perhaps the Holy Shroud was one of such '*convincing proofs*' Jesus offered his disciples to prove beyond a shadow of a doubt that he really had conquered sin and death through his actual, physical, bodily resurrection.

Not only for those disciples back then, but for those who would struggle to believe in the future.

"In recent years, there have been men," Jude Thaddeus continued, "evil, wicked men spawned from the loins of Satan himself, who are bent on deceiving the Church and driving from her the memory of Christ."

Alexander edged closer to the table, the phoenix stick

tattoo of intersecting lines rising to the surface of his consciousness.

Nous...

"These men," Alexander said. "What do they seek to destroy?"

"Why, the resurrection of Jesus! Stopping at nothing through all treacherous means necessary, they seek to destroy the proof that Jesus had offered his disciples. Nay, offered the Church herself! And the faith that flows from that powerful event. Exchanging the truth of who he is and what he accomplished for a heap of lies!"

"Why?"

"Because, dear fellow," Jude Thaddeus explained, "it is the 'why' of the Christian faith. It is why we were transformed from a bunch of petrified twentysomething boys and into men who gave our lives for a cause that challenged the might and power of both Rome and the Synagogue. Not turning from our Judaism, but turning toward the one who completed our Jewish story. And so we have provided reliable records of eyewitness accounts that a man from Nazareth, a man named Jesus and thought to be a prophet—*the* prophet, the new Moses—was crucified as an insurrectionist, a rebel against Empire Rome. And then he came back to life and was witnessed by hundreds of people. Including me and Simon, here."

Those tingles returned, raising the hairs on Alexander's arms and neck with amazement at sitting in the presence of one who walked and talked, lived and ate with Jesus—and who also witnessed his suffering on the cross and victory over the grave.

"That eyewitness testimony should be enough," Jude continued. "But..."

"But what?" asked Alexander.

The man sighed, his saggy, wrinkled cheeks billowing in protest. "But I wonder if it will be enough."

"How so?" Ford asked.

"You mentioned Thomas, dear fellow. A man who required physical proof, hard evidence that his friend, his Lord had truly risen from the grave. And I should say, *just as he promised he would*! Brother Thomas had to stick his fingers in the nail holes still crusted over with dried blood that marred Jesus' hands. Had to go poking around in his Lord's side where the spear cut loose the torrent of blood and water before he passed. And he did! At Jesus' invitation, mind you. Thomas went and took Jesus up on his offer for physical proof. Which did the trick. Brother Thomas stopped doubting the truth of the matter and was restored to belief. However, Jesus had some very telling words for him and all us disciples."

"*'Because you have seen me, you have believed,*'" Ford said. "*'Blessed are those who have not seen and yet have believed.*'"

Jude cocked his head and stared at him again. Alexander worried the man went too far this time in his recollection. None of those words from the twentieth chapter of John's Gospel would have been widely known during AD 65!

"Or so I've heard from one of the other disciples," Ford recovered.

"Really? Which?"

"Uh, don't recall." Ford glanced at Alexander and shrugged.

Jude Thaddeus continued, "Yes, well, at any rate I fear a day will come when belief will run as fleeting as in the very hours after news of Jesus' resurrection. The same kind of disbelief that plagued Christ's disciples."

Oh, that ship sailed long ago. Believe me...

A pain of regret wound its way up Alexander's spine at Jude's recollection of not only the events surrounding Jesus' resurrection, but also of what happened immediately afterward.

Doubt. Disbelief. Abandonment of reality.

"Which is why I secreted the cloth away and left it with Abgar for safekeeping," Jude Thaddeus said, "as well as something else."

Ford and Alexander glanced at each other, stiffening again with attention at the possibility. The final clue. The reason for their entire journey through time.

"And what was that?" asked Alexander, almost with a whisper.

The apostle grinned. "A *koinonia*."

"A koino-what?" Ford said.

Jude Thaddeus furrowed his brow with confusion. "Why, a community. A *brotherhood*. Are you sure you're from around here?"

"The Order..." Alexander whispered, not caring anymore what chaos Ford caused the space-time continuum with his slips of the tongue.

"What was that, brother?" asked Jude Thaddeus.

Alexander smiled and shook his head. "Nothing. You were saying something about leaving a koinonia, a community. In Edessa?"

"Yes. Wonderful men committed to contending for and preserving and fighting for the deposit of faith given to the Church by the Holy Spirit and committed by Christ himself through the apostles of our Lord. I fear that dark days lay ahead for the ecclesia. For those who bear the sign of the *ichthus*."

Ford and Alexander glanced at each other.

You have no idea.

"I just hope," Jude continued, "the brotherhood will continue what I started amongst them. Preserving what I and others passed along to them as of first importance. Sound instruction and right doctrine concerning Jesus' death on the cross for our sins according to the Scriptures, that he was buried in the tomb and was raised on the third day according to the Scriptures, later appearing to Peter and the rest of us apostles, then to even more people before ascending into the heavens. It would be my joy if the Church found a beacon of hopeful teaching radiating out from Edessa, guided by the rule for life and teaching I laid out amongst the brethren."

He paused to take a weary breath, then added, "At least the Order will always have a place of refuge, a source of encouragement and safety when the world goes dark—both inside the Church and outside throughout the Empire. Guarded by *sepio*, should you need it."

Guarded by sepio?

Alexander wondered what the apostle was getting at. Was it a person, or perhaps a code? He didn't get a chance to ask the man.

The apostle sighed, propping a cushion behind himself against the wall and leaning against it for support. The man looked like he was spent from the afternoon reminiscing of his missionary exploits and conveying his heart for the Church.

But there it was. What they came back to the past for, finding exactly what they needed.

Where it all began.

The tributary to the Order of Thaddeus, flowing out from Edessa and through history. Urging Ichthus to struggle and contend for the once-for-all faith delivered, committed, entrusted to the saints through the history of the Church. And it was a place of refuge for the Order when the world went dark.

Alexander just hoped what they needed for Ichthus back in the future was still there. He looked at Ford and nodded toward the door. Time to get to it. They went to say their goodbyes when Jude Thaddeus intercepted them.

"Before you go," he said, "I wonder if you might do us the honor of leading us in the Love Feast."

He grabbed the loaf and tore it in half, then offered it to Alexander.

The corners of his eyes brimmed with emotion at the notion. Take charge of the Eucharistic feast, with two of Jesus' disciples? He could get used to this time travel gig.

Alexander smiled. "It would be my honor."

CHAPTER 20

AFTER PARTAKING from the bread and cup, the Body and Blood of Christ, the men embraced. Simon and Jude Thaddeus made the two men from the future promise to keep in touch and seek them out again if they were ever in town.

Alexander threw Ford a knowing grin and told the men from the past they would try.

Saying their goodbyes, Alexander and Ford headed out into the evening. The sun was sinking fast toward the horizon, splashing a brilliant coat of burnt orange and crimson across a lightly clouded sky, the indigo water beneath reflecting back the majesty of creation. Long shadows from the beige buildings darkened their way as they hustled back to the garbage dump on the outskirts of town.

They kept silent and kept their heads down, weaving through crowded streets and alleyways, people reveling with song and dance and drink as evening inched toward the night-time hour.

When they were a safe distance, and Alexander could no longer take holding in the realization they had found their clue, he burst with a whisper, "Edessa! It's got to be the location of the remnant the way Jude Thaddeus was going on about the importance of the city for the Order. And it seemed like he offered some sort of shibboleth, a passcode to gain entry."

"Agree," Ford said, darting down the alleyway that clearly led back to the garbage dump, the humid smell of rotting waste slapping them in the face when they rounded the corner. "Edessa here we come, I guess. And I reckon *sepio* is an open sesame. Whatever that means."

Alexander winced and covered his mouth. "And if we're lucky, we may get a two-for-the-price-of-one deal for the effort."

"Yeah? What's that?"

"That Holy Shroud."

"You really believe in that thing? That not only was some sort of image left on the burial cloth of Jesus Christ, but that it was preserved by the early apostles and then preserved by this so-called Order of Thaddeus through the centuries?"

He did admit it all sounded like rubbish. Then again, both Luke and John recorded how Jesus had proved his resurrection to the disciples in various ways. Perhaps one of those was the Shroud.

Alexander answered, "Honestly, I'm not sure. But Jude Thaddeus sure was. And you heard what he said. The man brought a cloth along with him to Edessa. And this historical record from early Church historian Eusebius corroborates such a tale and image, along with countless other stories and verifications through the centuries. Only, the Holy Shroud has been lost for decades. Maybe it has returned to its home."

Ford said, "Alright, but why would it even matter now if it was in Edessa, along with some sort of remnant of the Order?"

"Think how much things have changed. And I don't just mean in Solterra, but in the churches spread across the Republic. People want scientific, existential proof for any sort of truth claim, let along religious and spiritual ones. I've seen it in my parish. At least, I did see it…"

Alexander stopped short, emotion catching in his throat at the reality of it all. He swallowed hard and pressed forward, the garbage dump coming into view at the end of the street.

"Anyway," he said, "people don't believe the eyewitness testimony of religious texts anymore. They certainly don't believe the historical, dogmatic teachings of an institution as storied as the Church. Ichthus means nothing to the world. Especially now that Panligo has basically dismantled it. I guess what I'm saying is, perhaps the Shroud was preserved for such a time as this. Perhaps this…relic, bearing witness to the essence of the Christian faith, could help us."

"Relics, shmelics," Ford grunted. "'*Blessed are those who have not seen and yet have believed.*' I take Jesus at his word on that one."

"Or, perhaps Jesus' actions spoke louder than his words when he offered up his nail-scarred hands as physical proof to even his doubting disciple that the central event of the man's faith was true."

"As those Frenchies from Europa say," Ford said, stopping at the edge of the garbage dump and turning to Alexander, "Touché, amigo. Got me there. Let's hope you're right on both counts. That holed up in Edessa is the remnant and the relic."

Alexander nodded. "How about we jump back home to find out?"

The men paused at the edge of the perimeter of the dumping grounds on the outskirts of town, taking in the area and searching for any watching eyes. Seeing and sensing no one, they hustled through the piles of refuse toward the hog-like mound that was guarding their way back to the future.

Alexander came upon it first. Blessedly, the broken shards

of pottery guarding the entrance to their gear were undisturbed. He cleared away the pieces and reached inside, sighing with relief and flashing Ford a grin of success. He quickly pulled out the belts, handing Ford his device.

The two strapped in, glancing around the site for anyone who might drop in on their exfiltration.

No one around. And not a sound but the lapping waves of the Mediterranean in the distance now darkened by the set sun, the bright white of the full moon lighting the world below.

Now to find their marker to ensure they jumped back to the right spot in the future.

Alexander stood just to the right of the boulder. Turning toward the town, he lined up his arm with the imperial statue gleaming from the moonlight to gauge the direction of their launch point back to the future.

He walked back toward the faded red amphora pot he had left as a landmark, lining up his steps and taking his time to get the pacing count right.

Eight, nine, ten, eleven...

Nothing.

No faded red amphora.

Alexander spun around, pivoting on his right heel and frantically searching the area for the landmark he had left.

Zip, zero, zilch!

Ford sidled up next to Alexander, folding his arms and shaking his head with a huff. "Told you so."

Alexander flashed him narrow eyes before looking around the ground for something, anything of landmark familiarity that would ground them for their return home.

None of it looked familiar in the moonlight.

"I'd offer you some seasoning to go along with that hat of yours," Ford said, "but I'm plumb out."

He ignored the man, his heart turning to ice and bowels

going weak with indecision and anxiety. Continuing his search, more frantic with each passing second, and coming up dry, his hand drifted inside his pants pocket. Without thinking, he withdrew the capsule of narcowafers, popped the top, and withdrew a ribbon of relief.

He slipped it into his mouth, his tongue pressing the wafer against the roof of his mouth, then he stuffed the capsule back inside his pocket.

And realized what he had just done.

Alexander whipped his head toward Ford, who had just turned toward the town, head down and searching.

Had he seen what he had done?

His head swam with the potent cocktail of synthetic narcotics and adrenaline-fueled panic.

What have I done...

"I think this is it," Ford announced, bending low to the ground.

Alexander startled, then heaved a breath and shuffled over to his side.

"How can you be sure?" he asked.

"These are pretty fresh tracks here in the—well, let's just say dirt for the sake of it. Because I don't want to think about what it might really be."

"Tracks? That's what you've got to go on?"

Ford looked up at Alexander looming over him, then stood and said, "Yeah, tracks. You know, the things people leave behind when they walk over said dirt while dumpster diving?"

Alexander rubbed the back of his neck and glanced around the ground. Looked about right. He scanned the surrounding area and back around toward the town again. Could be right.

"I don't know..." he said, returning to the ground.

Ford folded his arms. "Got any better ideas?"

He didn't. So he armed his belt for the return trip home.

"Let's just hope we don't end up next door in the ladies' restroom," Alexander said.

"Or in a wall."

"That too."

Ford followed Alexander's instructions for arming his own belt for the jump back to the future. All set. Two electromagnetic time travel devices ready to go.

They scanned the garbage dump one last time, then punched the blinking green *GO* button in Cyrillic and prepared to jump phases back to the future.

Lord Jesus Christ, Son of God, please bring us back home in one piece. And preferably back inside the men's restroom.

▭

BEIRUT, ARABIA-PERSIA. AD 2123.

The familiar undulating, vibrating waves began to take hold of Alexander's body, shocking him and warming him all at once as he zoomed through the bright luminescence at speeds he could only imagine. Every atom tingled with the familiar static charge, casting off the welcomed scent of time travel. He continued squeezing his eyes closed, concerned that if he opened them, his retinas would sizzle and his head would explode. He hoped Ford was beside him.

Then, as quickly as the warming vibrations and fluid tingles started, they all at once ceased. A feeling of levitation and weightlessness gave way to a heavy groundedness that felt solid under his feet. The bright light also dimmed to a faded darkness. Slowly, sound began to return to his silenced ears as well. The sound of lapping waves and squawking gulls, muffled yet close, relieved him.

As did the sight of Ford standing next to him when he eased open his eyes.

Alexander sighed with relief. His heart rate returned to normal, seeing them both standing in the bathroom they had left in their future phase.

The sound of a flushing toilet sent his pulse jolting forward and stomach to the tiled floor.

He snapped his head at Ford, matching his partner's startled wide eyes.

What the heck? They'd made sure no one was in the stall. Had locked the door solid. And Sasha said a few hours ticked by in the future world during jumps backward through time.

A stall door opened.

And a short, squat woman in a one-piece bathing suit with curly gray hair screamed with high-pitched fright.

They had jumped back to the women's restroom after all.

Without waiting for what came next after the scream, Alexander opened the door and darted outside with Ford hot on his heels.

A group walking past startled, exchanging glances between the two men and the still-screaming women's bathroom door.

"Our mistake," Ford said with a chuckle, holding up a reassuring hand. "Wrong restroom. Nothing to worry about, folks."

Alexander quickly tried the men's door, only to find it still locked.

Just the way they had left it. With the cases for their belts stowed inside.

Just great...

The woman emerged from the bathroom, slinging a string of words in a foreign tongue at the men and throwing a parting punch at Ford.

He ducked but got a one-two-three wallop on his back before she stormed off, shoes clacking down the boardwalk to safety. The group followed her, faces accusatory and twisted with disgust.

"We better get out of here like crap through a goose, partner, before Solterra mounties come a callin'."

Alexander couldn't have agreed more.

THE DIMLY LIT crypt pulsed with an almost holy hum as Dominic Weiss waited for his guest, an aura of sacred infamy surrounding the body resting in sweet repose beneath the marker above that countless pilgrims of Ichthus had venerated for centuries. A space that now served as ground zero for the systematic dismantling of the Church.

Which was entirely fitting, given the remains belonged to the man who had accidentally sparked its fractured demise over half a century ago.

Weiss knew better, of course. Knew it was merely the HVAC system regulating the humidity and temperature of the subterranean chamber, keeping the air cool and crisp for his use as a sort of headquarters for his operation. Knew that the sense of the sacred was merely an awareness of the freighted historical memory. Knew that feelings of religious affection permeating the chamber were more the product of the synapses in his brain than of any leftover holy halo belonging to the saint of Protestant Orthodoxy.

And yet, a part of him still held tightly to the truth that the holy and the sacred was real. Still held that it was invested in people and places and objects connected with the divine. Still held to the truth that a mystical power flowed through the veins of the Universe, tying every atom and molecule together in a harmonious unity, stretching from the beginning of time until now. A force that had been named and claimed by various sects across the expanse of time. Yahweh. Baal. Zeus. Jesus. Muhammed. Krishna. Buddha.

God.

Somehow, that force—that *idea*—had survived and thrived through the march of history, growing in strength and power through the Middle Ages and Enlightenment, modernism and postmodernism, and even in ultramodernity. And one iteration of that idea had perhaps the most shocking staying power of them all.

Ichthus. Christianity.

The Church, the Body. With Jesus Christ as its head, its font, its source.

Oh, the Universe had sure tried its damnedest to snuff the life out of it from the start before it could gain any sort of purchase in the space-time continuum.

Beginning with its prophet.

Crucifixions were expertly designed for such a purpose, used by Empire Rome to quickly suppress any sort of insurrection. Those Roman boards of execution that held the limp, lifeless bodies of countless insurrectionists made examples of all who would rise up and claim a kingdom that transcended Rome.

Just as Jesus of Nazareth had done.

'My kingdom is not of this world,' he had said when interrogated by the provincial prefect after entertaining claims questioning whether he was the king of the Jews. *'If it were, my servants would fight to prevent my arrest by the Jewish leaders. But now my kingdom is from another place.'*

Pontius Pilate didn't know what to make of this Jewish

prophet's crazy talk. So he finally relented and nailed Jesus to a cross, just like countless other terrorists had been, lining the roads into cities scattered across the Empire to remind the polis who was in control.

But then something curious happened. Something no one—neither the Roman officials nor Jewish leaders—could have anticipated.

The dead man came back to life again.

He resurrected from the grave. Like the phoenix myth of old.

It was a claim that quickly spread throughout Judea, so that the Jews manufactured a story about the disciples of the dead Jewish prophet stealing his body. Somehow (laughably) besting a legion of Rome's finest elite warriors. Decades later, the Empire blamed his followers for countless acts of misery, persecuting and killing them in droves.

Yet they persisted, persevered, remained faithful to their Lord, their King, their Savior.

At several critical junctures in Ichthus's life she could have been put down, hard and fast, like a rabid dog. Yes, there were the challenges from outside the Church—principally Rome, but also others who came along seeking the eradication of those who bent the knee to Jesus of Nazareth. Then there were the ones inside as well, the suppressed minority voices who sought an alternative understanding of the faith and challenged the elites within the Church who pulled the levers of power.

Nicolaism. Manichaeism. Gnosticism.

Marcionism. Sabellianism. Arianism.

Nestorianism. Pelagianism. And countless more *-isms* sprang up during the nascent centuries of the Church's existence to assert their perspective on the Christian faith and carry it into a new direction.

Yet something in the Universe carried the Church along,

steeling her and bearing her up while forces from within and without waged war. Always surviving, always remaining faithful to the original vision of God's will in heaven being done on earth through repentance from sins and faith in the death and resurrection of Jesus Christ.

And then it happened six hundred years ago, a millennium plus a half into her existence...

An arrangement of crimson candles bordering the sarcophagus flickered with an orange glow, their blood-red wax dripping onto the vessel holding the bones venerated by many and down to the stone floor beneath. Shadows danced around the space that had become a sanctuary for Cardinal Weiss beneath the narthex where he still commanded the attention of his parishioners from time to time. Though his newest venture prevented him from offering the same level of pastoral care he had offered the past few decades as priest of All Saints parish.

Weiss stood before the sarcophagus, taking a cautious step toward the rectangular, blockish object and spreading his palms upon its surface.

A chill ran through him, a shiver walked up his spine. Whether from the fruits of the ultramodern HVAC system regulating the climate or the sacred aura still emanating from within, he did not know. Dared not intuit.

Instead, he closed his eyes and took in a contemplative breath, considering all that the man inside had accomplished.

The great Martin Luther...

The match who'd lit the fuse that split the Western Church in two. Forever altering the course of Ichthus.

Although his original intent had indeed been a reformation of the Church, what his little act of protestant defiance accomplished instead was the wholesale *renovation* of the religion.

Weiss stood stiff and still, eyes closed and feet unmoving, feeling the aura surrounding the dead man pulsating from within the marble. Feeling a connection with the man inside. As if Weiss was Luther's doppelgänger, reincarnated for such a time as this.

And yet, he was altogether different.

He was no match.

He was a blowtorch.

The one who would burn Ichthus to the ground.

And from its rubble and ruin he would oversee the rising of a spiritual power far greater than had ever before been conceived. A true phoenix, rising from the bones and ashes of its dead ancestors to new life. Ready to lead a new incarnation of universal spiritual enlightenment and brotherhood that would bridge the ultramodern gap between the spiritual and the natural, between religion and science—ushering in a new era of higher consciousness of divine wisdom and endowing the individual with a deeper awareness of their inner divine spark.

A quote from the prophet Zarathustra rushed to the fore: *'You must be ready to burn yourself in your own flame; how could you rise anew if you have not first become ashes?'*

The sides of his mouth curled upward at the thought that he, Dominic Weiss, was the one the Universe had chosen to bear the flame that would set fire to the Church.

I am become flame
Destroyer of faith
Burning Ichthus to ash
For Humanity!

A buzz and then chiming chords drew his attention to his side pocket.

Weiss breathed deeply from the wonder at what he was on the threshold of accomplishing. He shoved off from Luther's marble tomb, the original flame-setter, and reached inside his cloak for the mobile device.

His pulse raced at sighting the caller hovering on its face.

Right on time...

One final loose end to snip before it would all be his.

"Is it done?" he snapped at his Ministerium contact.

There was hesitation on the other end before the caller said, "Unfortunately, no."

He closed his eyes and pulled in another stabilizing breath between clenched teeth. Now was not the time to erupt at the asset he had carefully cultivated the past year.

Opening his eyes, he simply said, "Explain."

"I followed the two men, Alexander Zarruq and John Mark Ford, from the Ministerium headquarters in Nicaea to Beirut, just as you instructed."

"Beirut?" he asked, his face twisting with confusion.

"That's right."

"But that doesn't make any sense. The city is the farthest thing from Ichthus friendly, a haven for radical Muhammedans and Solterra sympathizers, given the peace and economic security they brought to the region."

"I agree. It doesn't make sense. But that's not all of it."

"Go on," Weiss encouraged.

"I followed them onto a public boardwalk several blocks from the seaport," the caller explained.

"Followed them? Did they see you?"

"No. Not that I'm aware of. That wasn't the problem."

"Then what was?"

There was a pause on the other end, as if the person was working out an explanation.

Finally, they explained, "The two went into a public restroom adjacent to the boardwalk. I waited in the shadows to execute on your instructions. But here's the thing."

Weiss was growing impatient. "Spit it out already."

"The two men entered in through the men's restroom, but they came out of the women's side."

"OK…"

"They got into it with a female civilian outside. I waited for them to leave, then checked the men's restroom. It was locked, secure and tight. It was all rather peculiar."

"I should say so. Perhaps there was a door in between the two restrooms?"

"I thought that as well. So I busted through the lock and gained entry into the men's room. It was one complete room. Nothing in between. No door or window."

Weiss huffed with irritation. Where was this going?

"They also emerged," the caller continued, "or I should say stumbled, out of the women's restroom wearing some weird getup."

"What kind of getup? What were they wearing?"

"Not sure exactly, but it looked like belts of some kind. I didn't understand it. When I saw them go into the restroom, the *men's* restroom, they were carrying cases. A few hours later, they came back outside, from the *women's* restroom, without the cases and wearing the belts."

Weiss ran an impatient, irritated hand through his snow-white hair. None of this was making sense. The asset had been instructed to quietly put down the men who some others had identified working closely with Cardinal Ferraro responding to Panligo and securing Ichthus. Clearly that didn't happen. And now he was feeding him something about curious clothing and suspicious movement between restrooms?

But as irritating as it all was, none of it sounded right or normal.

The door clicked open, and the *click-click-click* of stilettos echoed through the crypt.

She's here.

"Stay on them," Weiss said.

"Already on it."

"Learn what they're playing at and keep me informed of anything else that develops. Then put the agents down. I want them taken care of before the morrow."

The caller gave Weiss reassurances then ended the call.

His guest arrived at his side, folding her arms and eyeing the surroundings. "Kind of a creepy place to call a meeting, Dominic," she said.

"Yes, well, I thought it best, given the nature of our rendezvous. Less possibility of Peeping Toms and all."

She nodded, saying nothing more.

Weiss turned toward the marble sarcophagus and cupped his hands, resting them in front. "*Hier stehe ich. Ich kann nicht anders,*" he announced, his clear, strong voice echoing throughout the space.

"Sorry, but my German's a little rusty."

He turned to her and smiled. "Do you know who is buried here?"

She frowned and shook her head.

"My, my. How is it you became part of the Ministerium security apparatus and don't even know the history of one of its central historical figures?"

"Was more of a sports girl than history buff growing up. And into guns instead of God."

"For some people, God and guns go hand in hand." He turned back toward the marble tomb. "'*Here I stand; I can do none other.*' Those were the words of Martin Luther, saint of Protestant Orthodoxy. The match that lit the Reformation. They were spoken at a tribunal in the Germanian town of Worms called to bring the monk to account for his trespasses against the Catholic Church of the day and answer their charges of heresy.

"With the threat of excommunication hanging over his head, and after days of testimony, he finally answered the crucial question: Would he or would he not recant? And this is what he said:

> 'Unless I am convinced by the testimony of the Scriptures and by clear reason (for I do not trust in the pope or councils alone, since it is well known that they have often erred and contradicted themselves), I am bound by the Scriptures I have quoted. My conscience is captive to the Word of God. I cannot and I will not retract anything, since it is neither safe nor right to go against conscience. May God help me. Amen.'

"Understandably, the room erupted with boos and jeers from the assembled group of Catholic officials inquiring of his heresies. And in the midst of the noise and chaos and din of the pandemonious reaction from his despisers, he said our Germanian words: 'Hier stehe ich. Ich kann nicht anders.' Here I stand; I can do none other."

"Interesting history lesson, prof. What's your point?"

Weiss turned to the woman. "My point is, neither can we. Neither can we do otherwise than our consciences dictate in light of the shifting, changing landscape of Solterra and Ichthus. In light of the advancements in our understanding of the Universe and the spiritual-natural interconnectedness of all things. The writing is on the wall. So here I stand; I cannot do otherwise."

He took a step toward her and took her hands in his. "My only question is, why are you standing? What is your interest in Panligo? It's a question that has been eating at me since you approached Apollos, and he arranged our connection."

The woman smirked. "I have my reasons."

Weiss went to say more when he noticed something on her wrist. He furrowed his brow and turned one of them upright. "What happened here, to the mark?"

Her face fell, and she jerked her hands away, folding her arms to cover up her wrists. "It's nothing."

"It's not nothing! You altered the mark. And into a Christian cross, of all things."

She reddened, embarrassed for the reason behind shaving the bent edges off the original marking of her employer. "I was caught. By that little weasel, Alexander. Had to improvise."

Weiss narrowed his eyes and nodded. "I understand. But I'm not sure the Thirteen will."

"I'll take my chances. Besides, they need me. You need me."

He offered a weak smile. "Yes, I do. And *we* need a drink."

Weiss turned away from the woman and walked toward a cart made of rare mahogany wood culled from even rarer wooden pews that had once been anchored to the floor above.

He uncorked a rare bottle of liquor and poured two-fingers worth of the sweet Germanian drink into two crystal tumblers.

The woman walked over, and Weiss handed her one, the candlelight glinting off the fine crystal etchings. She smelled it and raised a brow.

"What is this stuff?" she asked.

"Bärenjäger. A honey and bourbon liquor. It was rumored to have originated as a boozy bear lure used by eighteenth-century hunters and fur trappers. It's to die for."

"Well, then, 'For Humanity,'" she said, raising her tumbler with a grin.

Weiss raised his own glass, then simply smiled and took a mouthful, the fiery drink of oaky sweetness sliding nicely down his throat and instantly warming his belly.

Exactly.

FORD EASED the rented magnacraft across the parking lot and parked it in front of a dirty, squat beige box that stood the test of time. He powered it down, then stepped outside and whistled.

"This is the epicenter of vintage Christianity?"

Alexander stepped outside as well and frowned, disappointed that the cathedral, once dominating the region with Assyrian Christians living and worshiping in the ancient city formerly known as Edessa, looked more like a sad loaf of bread whose occupants had died out generations ago. A far cry from the gleaming beacon of hope that bore the torch of historic orthodoxy.

The smell of lemons mingled with herbs was the only bright spot on the property, a grove of them, watered and pruned, sitting toward the back. The lawn and gardens flanking the parking lot were unkempt and grown over, with weeds sprouting in eyesore clumps and a grouping of stone benches crumbling at the end of an overgrown path. Black mold streaked down the sides of the stone walls of the building, its facade pockmarked by age and neglect. Small windows were arrayed along the perimeter, darkened inside by paneling or curtains. Not a soul was around, neither coming nor going, and the surrounding neighborhood of ultramodern houses was still with sleep.

"Pretty well summarizes the state of Ichthus in twenty-second-century Solterra, doesn't it?" Alexander said.

"Word. At least they've got lemons to keep them company."

"You know what they say? When the Republic hands you lemons—"

"Chuck them back in their face?"

"Quiet, man. Never know who's listening."

Ford glanced around the property. "So Cardinal Ferraro thinks we're going to find what the Church needs to survive in this dump?"

Alexander shrugged. "Only one way to find out."

After the pair had made the jump back to the future, then emerged from the women's restroom and taken a beating from their surprised companion, they left the boardwalk and beach area in haste, grabbing cheap suitcases at a department store for their gear and finding a cheap hotel for the night with enough privacy to debrief with Father Jim.

He was ecstatic they had both survived, making another successful jump back into the early Church, and overwhelmed at what they had discovered. Not only the conversation they had had with Jude Thaddeus, but the potential lead with Edessa, now the Arabia-Persia city of Urfa and dominated by Muhammedans for centuries.

Ford expressed caution with putting too much stock in a single point of revelation. Felt like they were looking for a needle in a haystack and didn't want to get their hopes up. Didn't want to stretch the good Lord's goodwill after he had seen them through their time-travel ordeal.

Father Jim agreed, but reminded them of the Holy Spirit's movement as well. He was more than willing to pour out wisdom and direction with generous dosage on those who come empty-handed, which was the exact posture of the Ministerium. Figured the Holy Spirit's movement was about the only thing they had going for them, given the odds stacked against them inside and outside the Church.

The cardinal also figured Edessa made about the only sense of it, given its importance in the life of Jude Thaddeus and the Order of Thaddeus itself. He wished them the Lord's blessing for their mission and prayed his Spirit would guide them into the truth of the matter.

After the debriefing, they called Sasha before retiring for the night as well. The Ukrainski professor was ecstatic about their return. Couldn't wait to get his hands on the data inside the electromagnetic time travel devices. Begged them to take the first magnarail line to Kiev, but Alexander explained they had a side trip to the ancient city of Edessa beforehand. The man complained, and loudly, but relented. Told them "a nice bottle of Ukrainski candy" was waiting for them when they returned.

Signing off, they'd crashed hard and woke with a start at dawn's light struggling for attention behind the drawn curtains of their hotel window. They'd overslept and prayed to the good Lord above they hadn't missed their magnarail train.

Blessedly, they hadn't. Proving Father Jim right that God was more than generous with help in the midst of desperation.

Alexander hoped that generosity hadn't run dry. Because by the looks of things in Edessa, they were going to need a heaping portion of it.

He closed the door to the rental and led them toward a pair of wooden doors that anchored the front of the church. Their boards were rotting; the metal fittings holding the boards together were rusted and warped. Alexander feared the door would fall apart if he tugged it open.

Ford grabbed the handles and opened them anyway, the doors creaking mercilessly on rusted hinges, an ungodly echo sounding forth beyond.

The two men stepped through and were met with a set of thick violet curtains that formed an antechamber, thin whorls of silver threaded throughout.

"What do you make of it?" Alexander whispered on a shaky breath.

"Dunno. But now or never, partner. Let's roll."

He parted the curtain and pushed through; Alexander followed.

It was as if they stepped through the looking glass into an entirely different world, a stark contrast to the appearance the building offered on the outside.

Every inch was covered in gilt, shimmering and undulating in golden waves from hundreds, perhaps thousands, of lit candles splayed around the perimeter in banks of votives. A heavy, cloudy miasma of spicy incense hung stiffly in the warm, unmoving air inside. The space was cleared of the accoutrements you would normally expect in a cathedral nave: no pews or benches for sitting; no typical gilded high altar, except for a modest stone one up front; no instruments for worship.

And no people.

It was completely barren of life. Yet the hundreds of lit candles said otherwise.

Alexander approached one of the banks of candles, noticing tiny scraps of paper nestled under each of the candles. It looked like this was the case around the space. Curiously, they were all blank.

"What is this place?" asked Ford as he craned his head, mouth agape and eyes wide with wonder.

Alexander went to answer when movement caught his

attention near the front. He tugged on Ford's sleeve and pointed toward the figure, on the ground and bowed low.

They looked at each other with mutual confusion, then took cautious steps forward.

As they reached the middle, the figure slowly stood on shaky feet then turned around, revealing himself to be a frail man with bronzed, wrinkly skin hunched over a cane. Stringy gray hair ran down to his shoulders and his clothes draped loosely over a bony frame.

"May mercy be yours and peace and love in abundance!" the man said in Aramaic, opening his arms wide, his countenance gleaming with wide eyes and an even wider smile.

"Sounds like we found our guy," Ford mumbled. "Aren't those words from Jude Thaddeus's letter?"

He was right. Alexander's heart leaped with anticipation, eyes moistening with hope.

"Greetings," he said in the same tongue, the two men reaching the mystery man and offering a respectful bow. "May mercy be yours and peace and love in abundance as well." Then he chanced completing the circle of the apostle's letter: "To the only God our Savior through Jesus Christ our Lord be glory, majesty, power and authority, before all time, now and forevermore!"

"Amen!" the man said with holy enthusiasm. Then he leaned forward, resting against his cane with darting eyes, and whispered, "The epistle you've read and known, have you? Brothers in the faith, you are?"

Alexander glanced at Ford and flashed the elder a smile. "We have. We are. I am Alexander Zarruq, Bishop of Tripolitania. This is John Mark Ford, with the Ministerium. We come on behalf of the Fidelium, seeking your help."

"Christ be praised!" the man shouted ecstatically, offering an unexpected, eccentric hop. "And Theophilus am I."

"Quite the name you've got there," Ford said. "God-lover, is that right?"

"Your Koine Greek, you know. It is indeed. Call me Theo, as my friends do. The same you may do. Now, what is it I can do you for?"

Alexander took a breath and looked to Ford, who nodded him onward. He said, "We're looking for someone. Or *someones*."

"And find him or them here you think?"

He shrugged. "Not entirely sure. We were told by...well, a friend, that we could find a remnant of a certain religious order during desperate times. The Order will always have a place of refuge, a source of encouragement and safety when the world goes dark—both inside the Church and outside throughout the Empire."

The man seemed to perk up at the mention of this remnant and refuge.

Alexander glanced at Ford, then took a stabilizing breath for the true test.

The shibboleth.

"Sepio," Alexander said simply, eyes fixed on the holy man seeking a sign of recognition, of meaning.

"*Sepio*..." the man whispered, trailing off, before continuing: "Sepio, Erudio, Pugno, Inviglio, Observo."

Alexander immediately understood the Latin, his mind quickly churning out an interpretation.

So did Ford: "Protect, instruct, fight for, watch over, heed."

The man nodded slowly, then gasped with widened eyes that Alexander feared was a dying breath. Instead, he said, "You've come..." His eyes darted again, then he gave another hop and his face broke out in a grin. "You've come! The men in my vision, voicing the ancient shibboleth!"

"What vision?" asked Ford, glancing at Alexander.

"And who are you?" Alexander said with urgency.

"Why, Master of *Ordo Thaddeum,* I am."

Praise God! Alexander thought. They had found it. The lost Order of Thaddeus.

Ford whistled. "So it is true. The lost Order lives on."

"Lost it never was," Master Theo corrected. "In hiding, the remnant has been."

"Hiding? But why?" Alexander said.

The man's face fell, and he nodded solemnly. "Disgraced it was. And disbanded, but for the single office of Master."

"If I can ask, what happened?"

Theo shrugged. "What always happens when people care more about orthodoxy than they do orthopraxy. More about thinking rightly without marrying that with living rightly. Turned to the vices common to mankind they did: pride, greed, lust, envy, gluttony, wrath, sloth."

"The seven deadly sins," Ford said.

"Correct you are. Our founder, Jude Thaddeus, was concerned not only with the false beliefs being peddled by false teachers. Concerned about the kind of lives people were living as a result of those beliefs, he was. *'For certain people have secretly slipped in among you,'* he wrote, *'whose condemnation was long ago written about, ungodly people, those who pervert the grace of our God into a license to engage in outrageous, debauched behavior and deny our only Sovereign and Lord, Jesus Christ.'* A life lived in rebellion to the will of God is fundamentally linked to a heart that rejects the truth of Jesus Christ. About both Jude Thaddeus cared. As did our Lord and Savior, Jesus Christ."

Alexander considered this revelation. Then his mind leaped to the greatest command: "Love God and love people," he mumbled.

"Right you are. And a love for believing rightly must be

married to a love for living rightly. It is when doubt and unbelief overshadow the heart that wickedness is given a foothold. A quiet, peaceful space to work its dark magic in secret, producing all kinds of evil common to mankind."

"'*The light shines in the darkness, and the darkness has not overcome it,*'" Ford said, quoting from the first chapter of the Gospel of John.

The man smiled and nodded. "Right you are."

"Unfortunately, I'm not sure if John could foresee the advent of ultramodernity," Alexander said. "From my vantage point, darkness has indeed overcome the light. Where can we turn to rediscover the truth, Master Theo?"

"Dear fellow," the Order Master said, turning to Ford, "the bit you left out is where you find your answer. '*In him was life, and that life was the light of all mankind,*' Saint John said."

Alexander scoffed. "And where can we find such light, such clarity in these dark times? By my count, the truth of Jesus is confused now more than ever!"

The man grinned knowingly. "I will show you."

He turned around and hobbled toward an oversized religious icon anchoring the back of the nave just behind the stone altar. Alexander recognized it immediately. Christ the Giver of Life, the same one he himself had in the small chapel off to the side of his now-destroyed parish.

Master Theo dropped his cane to the ground with a clatter and grasped both sides of the icon's gilded frame. Then, with a strength Alexander was surprised the elder could muster, he hoisted it up and away from the wall.

Revealing a perfectly cut doorway and a darkened set of stairs leading beneath the chapel.

Ford whistled, the pitch of it echoing down into the maw of mystery.

Without waiting for their protest, the Order Master

retrieved his cane and one of the half-burnt candles, then started hobbling down into the void. The pair quickly followed.

"By the way, nice grove of lemons you've got out back," Ford said.

"Ahh, yes. Preserved for generations they have been," Master Theo said, inching down the stairs with care. "Planted by Jude Thaddeus himself they were."

"Well, I'll be."

Soon, they were standing in a small chamber with a low ceiling. And resting before them was a relic of Ichthus that was supposed to have been lost to history.

The Holy Shroud.

The cramped space was silent, yet it hummed with a holy presence and a sort of spiritual anticipation. The fourteen-foot beige cloth bearing the image of Jesus Christ was positioned beyond a single row of wooden pews in front of a small altar. A life-sized Christ-in-crucifixion of solid gold peered down upon the Shroud from behind.

Alexander caught his breath as he and Ford followed Master Theo toward the sacred relic, approaching the Shroud with cautious steps. He had been curious about the relic ever since hearing about it from Father Jim during his lecture. But it had been lost to history, never expected to have been laid eyes on again.

Until now...

The amber linen seemed to carry with it a special sacred glow in the candlelight, perhaps brought on by the gravity of their mission and the urgency of the memory it carried. The faint outlines of a man in sideways repose stared out at them. Dried blood, dark and crimson, was obvious on the forehead and back of the head, at each of the wrists and feet, and all along the arms and back and legs from hundreds of thin laceration marks.

A verse from the prophet Isaiah, chapter fifty-three, immediately sprang to Alexander's mind:

> *Surely he took up our pain*
> *and bore our suffering,*
> *yet we considered him punished by God,*
> *stricken by him, and afflicted.*
> *But he was pierced for our transgressions,*
> *he was crushed for our iniquities;*
> *the punishment that brought us peace was*
> *   on him,*
> *and by his wounds we are healed.*
> *He was oppressed and afflicted,*
> *yet he did not open his mouth;*
> *he was led like a lamb to the slaughter,*
> *and as a sheep before its shearers is silent,*
> *so he did not open his mouth.*

"Those marks there," Ford said, gesturing to a weird, patchy pattern mirrored on either side of the image. "What are those?"

"Burn holes and scorched areas they are," Master Theo said. "Caused by contact with molten silver during a fire in 1532 in the chapel in Chambery, France. Burned clear through the Shroud's linen while it was folded." He went quiet, face growing serious before continuing with reverent awe. "This tangible memory-marker of Jesus' physical, bodily resurrection was nearly completely destroyed were it not for a brave firefighter who rescued it from the clutches of Hades. And the sisters of Poor Clares convent repaired the linen by carefully sewing patches into the fabric to cover up the damage."

Master Theo stepped closer to it, pressing his hands against the glass. Then he said, "Carries the blood and sacred image of our holy Savior it does. A medieval forgery some have insisted. Rubbish that is!"

Standing face to face with the lost relic, Alexander couldn't have agreed more, believing without a shadow of a doubt that it was the genuine burial cloth of Jesus of Nazareth—who died, was buried, rose again, and was witnessed in bodily form by the very man who first formed the Church's first holy order.

"The faint imprint you see there," the Master explained, "is that of a real corpse in rigor mortis. The image is of a *crucified* victim. The blood you see there is real, actual dried human blood embedded in the cloth. And you can detect swelling around the eyes, the natural reaction to bruising from a beating. The New Testament claims Jesus was severely beaten before his crucifixion. Rigor mortis is also evident with the enlarged chest and distended feet, classic marks of an actual crucifixion."

Master Theo let that revelation settle before continuing.

"The man in that burial linen," he continued whispering, "was mutilated in exactly the same manner that the New Testament says Jesus of Nazareth was beaten, whipped, and executed by means of crucifixion. You have the scourging marks from a Roman flagrum on the arms, legs, and back. Lacerations around the head from the crown of thorns. His shoulder appears to be dislocated, probably from carrying his cross beam and falling. According to scientists who examined the Shroud, all of these wounds were inflicted while he was alive. Then, of course, there is the stab wound in the chest and the nail marks in the wrists and feet. All consistent with the eyewitness accounts recorded in the Gospels."

He turned around to face Alexander and Ford, whose eyes were misting with holy awe. "The image of the man, with all of his facial features and hair and wounds, is absolutely unique. Nothing like it in all the world. Totally inexplicable. And given there are no stains indicating decomposition on the linen itself, we know that whatever body was in the Shroud left before the decomposition process began. Just as the Gospel writers testify."

And then he dropped a bomb on them: "Here is your light. Here is the hope of mankind. Carry it with you into the darkened void of hell as a banner of truth. High time the Fidelium reclaim what is theirs it is."

"Wait, you're giving us the Holy Shroud?" Alexander said with disbelief.

Master Theo nodded. "Not only that, I am also—"

"Did you hear that?" Ford interrupted, spinning around toward the darkened stairwell and withdrawing his Sig Sauer.

Alexander's eyes went wide, his mouth went dry.

He said, "What did you—"

Ford hushed him, holding a finger to his mouth.

Alexander's heart began strumming a mean beat against his chest at the sudden shift. "Heard what?"

"Footfalls." He tilted his head back and to the side, sniffing the air. "And the smell of something burning."

The Order Master took a step forward. "They have arrived."

"Who's arrived?"

"The Church's nemesis stretching back to the earliest days of her existence. Come to destroy the Shroud they have."

Alexander and Ford looked at each other, nodding with recognition.

Nous.

CHAPTER 23

Ford trained his weapon on the darkened stairwell. Flickering orange light from the candlelight above washed over the stairs and began to grow with intensity along with tendrils of smoke reaching down toward the trio.

He took the stairs by two. Alexander was close behind but felt naked and exposed without his own weapon. The Order Master plodded behind him, the stump of his cane clacking slowly with each step.

The ex-Solterra soldier reached the top first and crouched, followed by Alexander, their backs against the cool brick growing warmer by the scene in front of them.

The life-size icon of Christ the Giver of Life was ablaze, its livid flames licking the wall and reaching toward the ceiling with threatening menace.

Ford glanced at Alexander, his face steely yet etched with the same concern that was racing through Alexander.

Someone had to have started the fire that was now threatening to overtake the entire chapel.

Ford nodded toward the nave then started forward, placing a careful step on the threshold of the stairwell and nosing his gun out before stealing a glance around the corner.

When he did, an arm shot out from his blind spot. It seized his weapon and yanked his arm with a stroke of precise training, throwing the man to the ground in one motion.

Ford tumbled forward before somersaulting and springing up with equally honed precision, his training with the Solterra Legion kicking into gear.

But it was no use.

A man Alexander didn't recognize was pointing Ford's gun back on him and commanding Alexander and the Order Master out of the stairwell.

Ford went to lunge forward when he was intercepted by the brute.

"Watch it Ford!" the man commanded, a jarhead in his own right, head shaved and wearing black with a mean scar stretching from mouth to ear.

Ford stood and raised his hands; Alexander followed his lead.

As the Order Master slunk behind the men, cowering lower for protection, something about the man struck Alexander as familiar

"The scar..." he murmured, recalling the guard he had noticed standing watch outside the conclave last week. The one who had burst through the double doors when Weiss and Nicolai and their crew infiltrated their gathering.

"You know this guy?" asked Ford.

"You don't?"

"Never seen him before in my life."

"Pretty certain he's part of your Ministerium security squad." With one hand he pointed at the man, the other he pointed at his own cheek. "Saw that scar on one of the Swiss Guards manning the conclave last week."

Ford took a breath and shook his head. Then he said to the

intruder, "You're part of Ministerium security, aren't you, jerkface?"

The man smiled and said nothing.

"That's crazier than a bare-naked bear in a berry patch."

"Alright, now that we've all gotten acquainted," the man growled. "How about we get down to business before the whole cathedral goes up in flames?"

"And what would that be, partner?" asked Ford.

The man shoved through the Ministerium men and grabbed the gray, stringy hair of the Order Master, yanking him out from hiding with a wicked scream and throwing him to the floor.

"He knows exactly what I want, don't you?" Training Ford's Sig Sauer on Master Theo, the hostile said to the two men, "And you'll go retrieve it for me, the burial linen of Jesus."

Took some doing, but ten minutes later, Ford and Alexander lugged the encased Holy Shroud up the stairwell and set it on the stone altar with a thud. Had no choice. The man threatened to blow off Master Theo's head.

"Ah, the Mandylion. The Image of Edessa. The Holy Shroud of your dead Jewish prophet." The man stepped forward, his weapon trained on the Order Master. He smirked and said, "For centuries, we tried to destroy the Shroud. Tortured one of its chief caretakers eight centuries ago, that dreadful Templars Master Jacques de Molay, but no dice. Came close a century ago, but it slipped through our fingers. Not today."

"And what do you intend to do with it now?" Master Theo asked, standing with defiance.

The man smiled, teeth crooked and stained. "Why, burn it, of course," he growled, eyes dancing with wicked delight. "Right after I blow your brains out."

Master Theo stepped up to the man, his face set as flint and back stiffening with resolve. "No such thing you will—"

The hostile whacked the elder across the head with his weapon, sending him to the floor in a slumping heap.

Alexander and Ford went to dart after the man when the hostile stepped back and waved his weapon at them. "I don't think so, fellas. Back off, unless you want to end up as the old man here."

He commanded them to kneel, lining them up next to the Order Master who was lying still on the floor, looking very much unconscious.

Alexander started shaking next to Ford, who was managing the situation with surprising calm. His heart hammered in his chest, his lungs screamed for more air, his head swam with dizzying fear as he waited for the inevitable.

He was going to die. His head blown right off in the middle of an ancient chapel in the armpit of Solterra.

He closed his eyes and clenched his jaw, sucking desperate breaths in through his nose, mouth quivering with a mixture of fear and anger and regret that it was ending like this.

"Who are you anyhow?" Ford asked facing forward along with the two other men, the hostile's boots squeaking behind them as he paced. "Solterra? Panligo? Nous?"

The man laughed. "Now, I do believe that word hasn't been spoken of in a century."

"So Nous, then," he said, trying to keep the man talking. "And, what, you infiltrated the Ministerium to steal a bedsheet?"

The hostile walked out from behind the line of men and stood to face Ford.

"You're a daft one, aren't you? Have no idea what is going on under your own two nostrils."

"I know you stink like a hog in heat," Ford said with a grin.

The man's face fell, his nostrils flared. He raised the weapon, the barrel inches from Ford's face. "The bedsheet wasn't my mission," he growled. "Just a consolation prize for getting rid of you two nosy—"

The weapon discharged with menacing purpose, a ricochet pinging off from the upper left wall behind them, startling Alexander with surprise.

Then again, mixed with a shout of anger and struggle for control.

Alexander threw his eyes open and twisted to see Ford kneeling with one foot planted firmly on the floor, holding the barrel of his weapon with one hand, the hostile's arm with the other.

The two were caught in a deathmatch for control.

And it wasn't clear who was winning.

With a passionate yell, Ford dropped his leg and leaned back. Completely changing the center of gravity of the exchange.

The hostile tumbled forward as Ford scooped the man up with his legs and sent him sailing over him in a heaping alley-oop tumble.

Losing the weapon in the process.

It skittered across the floor, landing in a pile of ash leftover from the smoldering religious icon.

The man recovered with ease just as Ford sprang to his legs. They crashed into each other, Ford's head low and back taking a wicked punch to his kidneys.

He responded in kind, slinging his hard head up the man's bottom jaw with a sickening crunch before headbutting him in the face.

The man yelped, his nose erupting in a geyser of blood.

"Hey, priest," Ford yelled, "could really use some gun-retrieving love right about now."

Alexander scrambled off the floor toward the weapon as the man recovered, landing a solid kick to Ford's solar plexus and sending him to the floor.

The hostile advanced as Ford tried to recover his breath.

"Shoot the bastard!" he groaned.

He grabbed Ford by the shirt and landed a strong blow to his face. Ford's own nose now erupted with slick crimson.

Alexander used his sleeve to retrieve the weapon, pushing the smoldering remains of the icon away. He grabbed it just as a fresh blow landed hard behind him.

But the butt was hotter than Hades.

He tossed it to the ground then whipped around, fearing Ford was dead.

But he was on top of the brute, landing another blow.

Alexander reached for the weapon again, his sleeve pulled over his hand as the men continued going at it. Holding it was now bearable.

He gripped it and took a cautious step forward, his hands shaking from the weight of the weapon and moment. He had never handled a gun before, much less shot one. Not only because of the Reckoning ban on an armed citizenry, but because he didn't believe in them on pacifistic principles.

And now he was advancing on someone with an outstretched arm bearing a weapon like those blasted Solterra security humanoids. The thought of killing a man made his bowels go weak.

The hostile spotted him with the gun and grunted. He struggled out from Ford's grip and landed a wicked kick to his jaw, sending him backward to the floor and well out of reach for any recourse.

He roared toward Alexander.

Then the gun went off. Didn't even remember pulling the trigger. But glad he did.

The bullet sank deep into the man's chest, blood instantly blooming and staining his dark shirt crimson. He stumbled backward, then faltered to one knee before going down hard on his side.

A tremor took hold of Alexander's arm holding the weapon. He let go of its butt, and it slid off his forefinger to the floor with an echoing clang.

The man rolled to his back, coughing blood before grinning widely with crimson-stained teeth. A giggle slipped through, then he said, "You think you've won..." He paused and heaved a desperate breath, his eyes going wide and face quickly draining of color. "Just you wait for—"

An explosion echoed wickedly at the back of the nave, cutting short the man's last dying words and echoing with evil intent. The ancient structure shook and roof groaned in protest before pieces started crashing to the floor below.

Ford didn't wait to process. He acted.

The man shoved off from the floor with a purposeful grunt. He grabbed the Order Master and shoved Alexander forward and through the opening leading down to the chamber below.

Sending both of them in a leaping dive out of harm's way.

Behind them, the ceiling began collapsing in a pluming cloud of dust and rubble.

Leaving the Order Master and Alexander trapped inside.

And Ford nowhere to be found.

CONTINUE READING SEASON 1

You've just finished episode 2 in the religious sci-fi apocalyptic thriller *End Times Chronicles Season 1*, the first book in the four-episode series, *Apostasy Rising*.

Think of it like your favorite Netflix, HBO, or Hulu show, where the story unfolds in installments. Each book can be read as a complete story with a beginning, middle, and end—but it ends on a cliffhanger that naturally flows into the next episode, fitting within a larger four-part tale.

Continue binge-reading the adventure by diving into the next episode now! Read a sneak-preview chapter of episode 2 on the next page. Buy on Amazon today:

APOSTASY RISING • Season 1

Episode 1
Episode 2
Episode 3
Episode 4

Building a relationship with my readers is one of my all-time favorite joys of writing! Once in a while I like to send out a newsletter with giveaways, free stories, pre-release content, updates on new books, and other bits on my stories.

Join my insider's group for updates, giveaways, and your free novel—a full-length action-adventure story in my *Order of Thaddeus* thriller series. Just tell me where to send it.

Follow this link to subscribe:
www.jabouma.com/free

***Group X Cases* Supernatural Suspense Series**

Not of This World • Book 1

The Darkest Valley • Book 2

Against These Powers • Book 3

Luck Be the Ladies • Novelette

***End Times Chronicles* Sci-Fi Apocalyptic Series**

Apostasy Rising / Season 1, Episode 1

Apostasy Rising / Season 1, Episode 2

Apostasy Rising / Season 1, Episode 3

Apostasy Rising / Season 1, Episode 4

Apocalypse Rising / Season 2, Episode 1

Apocalypse Rising / Season 2, Episode 2

Apocalypse Rising / Season 2, Episode 3

Apocalypse Rising / Season 2, Episode 4

Antichrist Rising / Season 3, Episode 1

Antichrist Rising / Season 3, Episode 2

Antichrist Rising / Season 3, Episode 3

Antichrist Rising / Season 3, Episode 4

***Faith Reimagined* Spiritual Coming-of-Age Series**

A Reimagined Faith • Book 1

A Rediscovered Faith • Book 2

***Mill Creek Junction* Short Story Series**

The New Normal • Collection 1

My Name's Johnny Pope • Collection 2

Joy to the Junction! • Collection 3

The Ties that Bind Us • Collection 4

A Matter of Justice • Collection 5

Get all the latest short stories at: www.millcreekjunction.com

Find all of my latest book releases at: www.jabouma.com

J. A. Bouma believes nobody should have to read bad religious fiction—whether it's cheesy plots with pat answers or misrepresentations of the Christian faith and the Bible. So he tells compelling, propulsive stories that thrill as much as inspire, while offering a dose of insight along the way.

As a former congressional staffer and pastor, and award-nominated bestselling author of over forty religious fiction and nonfiction books, he blends a love for ideas and adventure, exploration and discovery, thrill and thought. With graduate degrees in Christian thought and the Bible, and armed with a voracious appetite for most mainstream genres, he tells stories you'll read with abandon and recommend with pride—exploring the tension of faith and doubt, spirituality and culture, belief and practice, and the gritty drama that is our collective pilgrim story.

When not putting fingers to keyboard, he loves vintage jazz vinyl, a glass of Malbec, and an epic read—preferably together. He lives in Grand Rapids with his wife, two kiddos, and rambunctious boxer-pug-terrier.

Connect at: www.jabouma.com • jeremy@jabouma.com

facebook.com/jaboumabooks

twitter.com/bouma

amazon.com/author/jabouma